END OF THE LANE

A Dear Abby Cozy Mystery - Book 1

SONIA PARIN

ISBN: 1983856673

ISBN-13: 978-1983856679

"If I had to do it over again, I would use a knife instead of the scissors. I now realize it would have been more dramatic but I got caught up in the spur of the moment and it was all I could think of grabbing. Don't get me wrong, I'm not a violent person..." Abby's voice rose above the latest news report announcing the discovery of yet another body. That made it two within the last three hours.

"Someone's been busy." She changed radio stations only to find more of the same.

... Police have yet to confirm the identity of the latest victim or make any comments about the similarities...

A serial killer on the loose? "So just be on the lookout for anyone acting suspiciously," Abby said in a sing-song tone, now more than ever becoming aware of the isolated stretch of road she'd been traveling on.

Seeing a car approaching, she told herself to look the other way, but a mixture of instinct and curiosity took over. "Red pickup. Male driver wearing a blue baseball cap. Scruffy looking. Nothing but your average looking suspicious person." She took note of the time for good measure and, brushing a hand across her face, decided she'd been on the road for too long. Worse, she'd been talking to herself for hours now.

Unclenching her jaw, she smiled at the crusty ball of fur she'd picked up a few miles back. The dog watched her in silence. "Don't worry, I'll get you back to your owner as soon as I figure out where to start looking."

The last time she'd checked the road map she thought she'd seen signs of the end of her journey, but according to the GPS in her new second-hand car...

"Hang on. I think that's a sign up ahead." Abby leaned forward. "Yes. Welcome to Eden. Population 2,153. Soon to be 2,154. This is it. The end of the line for me. The town where no one knows my name. This is your fresh start, Abby Maguire. From here on in, everything will work out for you exactly as planned. With no surprises, thank you very much." She'd had enough of those to last her a lifetime.

The pregnancy test kit... Not hers.

The sudden dip in her shared savings account. Not her doing.

The velvet case with a sparkling diamond ring. Not for her.

Shredding her ex's favorite suit...

Abby grinned. She'd definitely had a hand in that.

Unfortunately, the run of bad luck hadn't stopped with her private life. The newspaper she'd worked for in Seattle had been sold to the highest bidder leaving more than half the staff out of a job.

Again, not her doing.

"This, however, is entirely my doing." Her bright idea. A complete sea change. And why not?

"A job is a job and countless newspaper moguls began their careers in a small-town press." Not that she had illusions of ever taking over the world.

While her sights had never been aimed very high, she'd always managed to work for major newspapers or magazines. Now... Abby decided there was something adventurous about doing the complete opposite to what she should be doing.

Abby spotted a building up ahead which turned out to be a derelict looking house. She glanced down at the dog. "Do you remember if that man at the last gas station we stopped at mentioned anything about an old house as a landmark? Yes? No?" He hadn't said much. In fact, he'd been too engrossed with the news breaking over the airways to pay any attention to her.

Abby shivered. "One of my first jobs as a reporter involved covering a murder trial. I found the experience gruesome enough to put me off for life." The stray huffed out a breath and rested his chin on his paws. "Back then, I'd been on a lucky streak and managed to make an effortless move to a lifestyle magazine to write about celebrity house makeovers." She glanced down again. "What? Not impressed. This newspaper job I've lined up for myself won't be glamorous, but I'm looking forward to a quiet break writing feature articles about the weekend's bake sale and interviewing locals for the face of the town series." Abby grinned. "I pitched the idea during my phone interview." And it had sealed the deal for her.

"Hey... here we are. Blink and you miss it. So, pay attention." As her new stomping ground came into view, Abby slowed down, although a part of her urged her to put the pedal to the metal and keep going. "Oh, look. A café. That means coffee. No need to panic." She smiled and immediately perked up.

The main street looked like any regular town with a variety of stores including a hardware store, a café and a couple of restaurants, a grocery store and, her destination, a pub.

She could not have missed it even if she'd tried. Painted fire engine red, it had what looked like a ship's figurehead hanging next to the main entrance. The Gloriana had been the only place offering rooms. The alternative had been a bed and breakfast just outside of town, but that had been fully booked.

"First thing first. I'll shake off my jet lag with a wander around the town and then..." She looked down at the stray dog curled up on the passenger seat. His large brown eyes peered up at her. "Okay. Slight revision to my plans. First thing on my to do list is to find the local vet and have you checked over. Who knows how long you've been wandering around lost?" She reached down and gave him a scratch behind the ear and was rewarded with a lick. "After that, I might as well present myself at my new job." The Eden Rise Gazette. It had a nice ring to it. Like a burst of sunshine to cast away the gloom that had been hanging over her head these last few months.

Pulling up outside the pub, she gathered the stray in her arms, and stopped the first person walking by to ask for directions to the nearest vet's clinic.

"... Across the street. Next to the Gazette..."

Perfect. "See Buddy, things are falling into place for us." The stray answered with a slight quiver. "We'll get you sorted out in no time."

Seeing the Eden Rise Gazette, she slowed down. It looked like a regular store with large windows facing the street. As she strode past it, Abby glanced inside. Wood paneled walls were covered with framed news articles. A young woman sat behind a desk talking with a man in a dark gray suit. Their eyes connected briefly. The woman smiled, but it looked distracted.

When they came up to the clinic, the stray gave a little whimper as if sensing they'd arrived at a place he didn't much care for. Inside, an elderly woman was being reunited with her cat, Smidgen, and a young man sat in a corner, his dog curled up between his feet.

"Hello, what have we got here?" The receptionist came around the desk.

Abby tucked a loose tendril behind her ear, a habit she'd often tried and failed to break. "I found this little guy by the side of the road. He looked exhausted. I'm guessing he's a long way from home and hasn't had any food in a while." Feeling a slight twinge of reluctance, Abby handed him over. "I've been calling him Buddy."

"If he belongs to a local he'll have an ID chip. Hang around a sec, I'll take him through and I'll come back and get some details from you."

A few minutes later the girl reappeared. "Pete Cummings, that's the vet, had a quick look. No broken bones. No signs of external injuries, but he looks dehydrated. He wants to keep him overnight. We'll clean him up for you." The girl smiled at her. "I haven't seen you around here before. Are you passing through?"

"I'm actually new in town. I'm Abby Maguire. I'll be working at the Eden Rise Gazette next door."

The girl introduced herself as Katherine. Her short crop of hair mirrored Abby's, right down to the same shade of chocolate brown. "Do you want us to contact you about him?"

"Yes, please." She wrote down her cell phone number and left thinking it would be nice to see what Buddy looked like underneath the layers of crusty mud.

Outside, she took a moment to gather her thoughts.

Her body and mind remained on a different time zone 8300 plus miles away. Less than a day ago she'd been sipping a coffee in Seattle. Now... she looked around the small alpine town of Eden and thought about the research she'd done online.

The highest mountains in the state were found here boasting stunningly beautiful views with dramatic mountain landscapes, wild rivers...

Fantastic if you liked the great outdoors.

She'd arrived in mid-season. In a few weeks, winter would settle in and the local ski resorts would start their roaring trade. Of all the places she could have landed in Australia, land of beaches and sparkling sunshine...

Abby smiled to herself. If she wanted beaches, she could have them by hopping in her car and driving for three hours. Right now, this was it. Home away from home. With a slight time difference and, so far, no rain...

If she checked in at the pub now, she'd collapse and sleep until who knew when. Deciding to keep herself awake until a more reasonable hour, she went into the newspaper office.

The young woman she'd seen talking to the man in a suit was now on the phone. She looked slightly flustered, her eyebrows drawn down, her lips pressed tightly together. Seeing Abby, she disconnected the call.

Abby hoped she hadn't arrived at a bad time. Smiling, she introduced herself.

"We've been expecting you. I'm Faith O'Keefe. Dermot left instructions to send you straight to his place when you arrived. He's been working on his memoir and doing research at home."

Dermot Cavendish, the owner of the newspaper, had given her the job a day after she'd applied for it, while the one hundred and twenty-seven other job applications she'd sent out to various other newspapers, including her home town one in Iowa, remained unanswered.

"Does he live nearby?"

"You can walk to his place in under five minutes. I'll draw you a map. If you like I can give you a tour of the office first. Although there's really not much to it. In fact, this is it."

Filing cabinets lined one entire wall. A large desk, probably antique or at least as old as the building, sat at one end, while a large table, another antique, by the looks of it, with newspapers and magazines stacked in neat piles, occupied most of the remaining space.

"The printing room is at the rear. The weekly issue comes out on Fridays..."

That gave Abby a few days to get settled. She looked around the quaint looking space with its store-front facing the street.

For years, she'd worked in a high-rise building. Being eye level with the pavement would be a welcome change.

"There's a lot of foot traffic and we get people dropping in all the time."

And waving as they walked by, Abby noticed.

"Dermot mentioned you've worked in a large newspaper. The slower pace will probably take some getting used to. I hope it doesn't put you off. He's been thinking about retiring for a long while now. I think having you here is his way of easing back and slowing down." Faith got busy writing down the directions for her. "Here you go. It's straightforward. You can't miss it, just think of Edgar Allan Poe."

As she strode along the street, Abby wondered how much of today she'd remember. She'd barely slept a wink during her twenty odd hour flight and wouldn't be surprised if she woke up the next day in a daze.

"And in desperate need of a coffee." She sent a silent prayer to the Gods of Caffeine. If the local café couldn't provide her with a decent cup, and by that she meant something that conformed to the standard she'd become accustomed to, she'd have to rethink this entire adventure. She didn't ask for much, but there were some essentials in life she couldn't do without.

Checking the map Faith had given her, she counted three turns. She'd drawn an open book in one corner to signal the first turn.

"Paige's Bookstore." Abby stopped for a moment to look at the window display. Her attention bounced between a book that caught her interest and the reflection on the window of people striding by.

Abby nearly caved in to the temptation to double back and find a café, take time out and refuel before meeting her future boss. Instead, she forged ahead.

As she stepped away from the bookstore she

collided with a woman hurrying by, her shoulder connecting with hers.

"Sorry," she offered.

The woman grunted something incoherent and straightening her pale blue jacket, she hurried off.

Quaint Victorian houses were lined up one next to the other along Edgar Street. Abby turned into Allan Street and decided this had to be the older part of town with cobbled streets and...

"A strange sense of humor. Take a right into Poe Lane and keep going until you reach the end of the lane." Faith had been right. Just think of Edgar Allan Poe. Ironically, she saw a raven swoop down and fly off.

Abby wished she'd taken a moment to run a comb through her hair. She'd spent most of the drive here raking her fingers through it, worrying and wondering if she'd made the right decision. The contract had been signed, so she'd already made the commitment to spend the next twelve months here, far away from everything and everyone she knew.

Reaching the house, she was about to knock on the front door but hesitated when she saw it was partly open. Abby looked around her but didn't see anyone on the street and there weren't any signs of activity such as gardening tools lying around in the postage stamp sized garden. "Maybe Dermot Cavendish stepped out for a moment and the wind blew the door open," she said under her breath.

Except... there wasn't a lick of wind.

"Hello," she called out. The windows were open and she could hear a light piano tune playing in the background. It sounded familiar but she couldn't put her finger on it. Giving the door a slight nudge, she called out again.

The tune ended. Abby listened to the silence. She took the opportunity to knock on the door again. "Hello, Mr. Cavendish. It's Abby Maguire. We spoke on the phone a few days ago. I'm the new reporter at the Eden Rise Gazette." She didn't know why she'd thought to tag that last bit on. Dermot Cavendish was well into his eighties, but the man she'd spoken with had been sharp witted and eloquent.

Abby looked at the neighboring houses and wondered if he'd stepped out to visit a neighbor.

If she'd been watching a movie, Abby would have screamed at the screen. "Whatever you do. Don't go in." Because the moment she did, Dermot Cavendish was bound to appear and probably think she'd been snooping around. Or worse. What if she caught him by surprise and gave him a heart attack?

Abby's toes curled inside her boots.

One quick peek inside won't hurt.

"He might be sharp witted but he is eighty plus," she reasoned. What if he'd fallen?

Scooping in a big breath for fortitude, she eased the door open. "I'm coming in, Mr. Cavendish," she called out. Another thought struck. What if he'd slipped and fallen in the shower? That would make an awkward first encounter and set them off on the wrong foot.

She took a couple of tentative steps inside and sent her gaze skating along the bookcases lining the narrow hallway. To her right, a set of double glass doors opened to a sitting room. As she strode in, a floorboard creaked beneath her feet. In that split second, she looked down only to whip her gaze back up.

"This does not look good," she whispered. Her heart gave a hard thump followed by an urgent hammering against her chest.

Dermot Cavendish sat on an upholstered armchair, his head tilted to the side, his mouth gaping open. She knew it was Dermot because she'd seen photos of him when she'd researched the job. Abby settled her gaze on his chest and held it there for several seconds waiting to see it rise.

It didn't.

"This doesn't look good at all." Her voice shook, right along with her fingers. She drew out her cell and dialed 911 only to remember she wasn't back home. "Think. Think." She'd skimmed through some basic information during her flight. Contrary to popular belief, kangaroos did not roam freely through the streets. Also, cars were driven on the left-hand side and the steering wheels were on the right-hand side. The country played host to the deadliest critters around. Spiders. Snakes. Even octopuses with pretty yet deadly blue rings.

Among all that information, there had been a list of emergency services.

Her gaze bounced between her cell phone and Dermot Cavendish. She still couldn't see his chest moving. But she had to be sure. Even as she did a quick search for the local emergency number, she pressed her fingers against his neck.

She stood there gazing at his vacant eyes and then stepped back and dialed 000.

The sound of a distant voice pulled her out of her stupor.

The operator asked which emergency service she required. A simple enough question. For someone who made a living out of playing with words she suddenly struggled to think of anything appropriate to say. "I think he's dead. In fact, I'm sure he is."

Abby took a few stumbling steps back until she came up against a wall. She looked around the room as if searching for something. Although what, she had no idea.

Her new employer... dead.

Chapter Two

_a_bby held something warm, comforting and familiar between her hands. She must have looked puzzled because she heard someone say, "Coffee." Abby looked up. "Smells good."

"It's from Joyce's Café. She calls it _Wake Me Up Before the Sun Comes Up_. She made me say it three times so I wouldn't forget. Just in case you liked it and wanted to order it again."

"Thank you." Her voice sounded croaky. Abby took a sip. "Joyce's Café?"

"Around the corner. On the main street. You can't miss it. Just follow the aroma of coffee."

That sounded reassuring. She took a longer sip. "I believe it's about to become my home away from home. This is very good."

"I'll tell Joyce you said so."

Abby drank half the coffee in one gulp. "Sorry, I

didn't catch your name."

"Detective Inspector Ryan."

"I'm Abby Maguire."

He gave her a small nod. Abby couldn't remember if she'd already introduced herself. The last hour or so had become a haze of too many things happening at once. Her lingering jet lag had completely annihilated her reporter's instinct. She had a vague memory of the police arriving along with the ambulance and of being escorted out of the sitting room and into an adjoining book lined room. Everyone had spoken in hushed tones. She also remembered seeing a couple of people dressed in white jumpsuits. Crime scene investigators, she assumed.

Abby looked around the room she sat in. Every available wall space was covered with floor to ceiling bookcases. In all the time she'd been sitting here, she hadn't picked up a single book, which said a great deal about how she felt.

"Are you up to talking?" the detective asked.

"Dermot Cavendish? Is he...?"

The detective nodded. "His body has just been removed."

He hadn't left. He'd been removed. No, not him. His body had been taken away and he'd become ethereal. Yet in her mind, he remained Dermot Cavendish, the man she'd traveled half way around the world to work for.

"He'd been expecting me. I've only recently arrived

in the country, but I'm on a different time zone so I'm still trying to adjust." She knew she was rambling, but now that she'd started talking she couldn't stop. "I thought I'd come by to introduce myself. I'm... well, I was the new reporter at the Eden Rise Gazette. My first assignment was going to be this weekend's bake sale. I'm... I was supposed to find a story somewhere about Lamingtons."

The detective nodded. "The Lamington saga. It's been going on for ages."

Lamington saga?

He cleared his throat. "Do you remember what time you arrived?"

Abby forced herself to focus. "Before midday. My flight arrived at six this morning. It took me about an hour to get through customs and collect my new car. Well, not really new, but new to me. I purchased it online. Then I drove here." She gazed at him and had the strangest feeling he was humoring her. Or worse. She was giving him too much information. She hoped he didn't take that as a sign of guilt.

Guilt?

"It's a three-hour drive from Melbourne," he said.

"I drove slowly. I'm not used to driving on the left-hand side, so I had to take extra care. Then I stopped." She pressed the cup to her lips. "I picked up a dog." She saw the detective frown. "Did that sound odd? It sounded odd to me. Like something out of sequence. Anyhow, I arrived in Eden and took the stray, Buddy, to the vet." She gave a small nod as if to confirm what had happened. She hoped she hadn't imagined it because then that would mean she'd stepped into some sort of Twilight Zone episode where no one would believe her. Abby shifted in her chair. "When I called the ambulance I'd only been in the house a couple of minutes. I'm sure they'll be able to verify the time."

"What about when you entered the house. Did you hear anything? See anyone?"

"No, the place was empty... except for Mr. Cavendish. At least I assume it was. I didn't move away from the room where I found him." She frowned. "When I arrived I heard music playing. A piano tune. Then it stopped. If that helps..."

He made a note of it.

She leaned forward and looked across the hallway to the sitting room where she'd found Dermot. "Was it a CD?"

"Why do you ask?"

"If you look at the running time, you'd get a rough idea of when he'd been alive."

"What sort of reporter are you?"

"Lifestyle." Although, she wouldn't be able to describe the room she'd been sitting in to save her life. Her mind had simply shut down. "Dermot Cavendish thought I'd be a perfect fit for his small newspaper." She drank the rest of the coffee and wondered if she'd already told him that. Blabbering. That had to be a sign of guilt...

"Would you like another coffee?"

"No, thanks." She twirled the empty cup in her hands. "I can't even remember if I saw cars driving by. There must have been. I encountered a few people along the way, but I can't say that I noticed anything or anyone in particular." Forgetting she'd drunk her coffee, she lifted the cup to her lips. "He'd been drinking tea." She closed her eyes and tried to remember why she knew this. "I think I saw a teapot on a small table beside his armchair."

"Lukewarm."

"Pardon?" she asked.

"Nothing."

"What happens now?" she asked.

"It's up to the coroner."

"What does that mean?"

"Cause of death needs to be determined. Especially if there is no pre-existing illness."

"So, there might be an autopsy?" she asked.

"His next of kin needs to be informed first. Until then, we'd appreciate it if you didn't mention this to anyone."

"Am I free to go?"

"Yes. How can we contact you?"

She gave him her number. "I'm staying at The Gloriana."

The detective walked her out of the house. The sun had disappeared behind a cover of puffy clouds, but the sky didn't look threatening. If anything, she felt over-

dressed for the mild weather. Abby ┌
of her sweater up to her elbows and
pace, her thoughts in stasis. The momen┌
the pillow, she knew she'd fall instantly asleep.

When she reached her car, she grabbed her sr┌
suitcase and headed straight to the pub. Lunch service
appeared to be in full swing. Conversation and music
mingled.

"G'day."

She smiled at the sound of the typical Australian
greeting. "I have a booking. Abby Maguire." The man
stood a head taller than her. He had bright blue eyes that
sparkled with a hint of mischief.

"We've been expecting you. I'm Mitch Faydon."

She gave him a small smile, all she could manage
considering her sleep deprivation and shock.

"Is that all your luggage?" he asked.

"No, the rest is in my car. I'll get it later." After
she'd settled in. Abby raked her fingers through her hair.
Then again, her stay might just have been cut short.

Mitch Faydon took her suitcase and said,
"Follow me."

The pub had the air of a hunting lodge with trophies
and rifles hanging on the walls along with a large
display of black and white and sepia colored
photographs. A large stone fireplace sat at one end with
a couple of comfy high-backed chairs positioned with
enough room to stretch out and drink at leisure. The
walls surrounding it were all wood paneled.

he stairs creaked under her feet. Abby brushed her
gers across her forehead as she remembered striding
a to Dermot Cavendish's house and stepping on a loose
floorboard.

"Here we are."

The room looked comfortable in a homey sort of
way with more perks than the average hotel room. "This
looks like a deluxe room." Or a private apartment.

Mitch Faydon smiled. "Dermot called us to say we
should make you feel welcome and comfortable."

"How kind." The words caught in her throat. She'd
promised to keep quiet about Dermot. The truth would
eventually come out and Mitch Faydon would know
she'd withheld the news.

"If you need anything, just pick up the phone and
dial one. Either I'll pick up or one of my brothers will.
If you hear a deep grumble, don't be concerned. That's
just my brother Markus. We're still house training him."
He gave her an easy smile. "I'll leave you to it."

"Thanks."

As soon as the door closed, Abby collapsed on the
bed face down and moaned. Annoyingly she laughed as
she recalled wondering if she'd remember anything
from that day. How could she ever forget starting this
new chapter in her life and finding it might actually
come to a premature end before she could live to regret
her decision?

The thought faded and she dozed off.

Chapter Three

The incessant ringing of her cell phone pulled Abby out of a deep slumber. Peeling one eye open, Abby looked at the caller ID but didn't recognize the number.

"Hello?" Abby mumbled.

"Abby, it's Faith. Faith O'Keefe from the newspaper. We met this morning. I just heard what happened."

"What happened?" Abby asked, her voice still in slumber mode.

"Dermot's gone..."

Abby rolled onto her back. Dermot Cavendish. Dead. "Dreadful news," she managed to say as she rubbed her eyes. "How... how did you find out?"

Faith hesitated. "A neighbor stopped by and told me about it. She saw everything."

"Which part?"

"The police and ambulance arriving. That was

enough to alert everyone. We're all in shock. No one ever imagined this could happen here."

Abby supposed the police would eventually do a door-to-door sweep of the area to ask if anybody had seen anything or anyone.

"Any idea how it happened?" Faith asked.

"I couldn't say. I walked in and there he was, on the armchair." She brushed her hand across her face. There had been a pot of tea on a small table and... a cup. A cup and saucer tipped over on the floor. Had she mentioned that to the police? No, of course she hadn't because she'd only thought about it now. "Did he have any family?"

"His grandson. The police dropped by a while ago to get his contact information. They told me not to talk to anyone but I figured it would be okay to call you since you're the one who found him."

"How do you know that?"

Faith sighed. "The neighbor. She noticed you standing outside Dermot's house."

Abby brushed her hand across her face again. She felt bleary eyed and thirsty. Sending her gaze skating around the room, she spotted a small refrigerator and tried to will herself to move but couldn't quite manage it. "Did she also happen to notice the killer?"

"So, he was killed."

"I didn't say that," Abby backpedaled as fast as she could. How could she have let that slip?

"Yes, you did."

Why had she? Abby frowned up at the ceiling and then remembered the police wearing white jumpsuits, crime scene investigators, she thought, there to gather forensic evidence. "Forget I said it."

Faith laughed. "That's silly. It's like in those films or TV shows were the judge instructs the jury to disregard the remark made by the lawyer or the witness, never mind that it always happens to be something significant. How exactly is someone supposed to forget something they just heard?"

Easy, Abby thought. "Don't think about it." She rolled off the bed and made a beeline for the refrigerator, her mind focused on getting some water.

"Hard to do when it's all anyone can talk about."

Abby groaned lightly. She tucked the bottle between her legs and twisted the cap off. "How are you holding up? The news must have come as a shock to you."

"It hasn't sunk in yet. I expect him to walk in through the door any minute. I guess I'm in denial." Faith's voice shook. "I've worked for Dermot for six years. He gave me my first job. Now..." Faith huffed out a breath. "This will probably sound insensitive, but I've no idea what I'm going to do. Jobs around here don't crop up every day."

"You think the newspaper will close?" Abby asked.

"Most likely. His grandson has never had any interest in keeping it running. The last time he came to visit Dermot, they argued. He wanted Dermot to retire and go live in the city."

"What does he do?"

"He owns the Daily First, it's a national newspaper."

Abby frowned then mentally smacked her hand against her forehead. Sebastian Cavendish owned the Daily First. She'd known Dermot had been at the helm years before but had since stepped down to focus on the small town newspaper. Why hadn't she made the connection before now?

It wouldn't take a genius to figure out Sebastian Cavendish wouldn't be the slightest bit interested in a small-town press.

"Are you all right?" Faith asked.

"I'm... Yes. Yes, I'm fine." These last few months had been a whirlpool of chaos. She hadn't been thinking straight long enough to realize Sebastian and Dermot were related. There'd been a rumor flying around about Sebastian's global conglomerate being behind the takeover of the newspaper she'd worked for in Seattle...

"It's the end of an era," Faith said, "Dermot's grand-father founded the Eden Rise Gazette. It's how the family got into the newspaper business. Now we'll have to close the doors."

Without the Gazette, there would not have been a Daily First and Dermot's grandson might never have gone into the business, Abby guessed. "Maybe the grandson will keep it running for its sentimental value or sell it as a going concern."

"I wish. But who'd be interested in buying some-thing that doesn't turn a profit. A couple of years ago,

Dermot made the gazette free. There's no coming back from that."

"Don't worry, Faith. As the saying goes, it might never happen."

"You think Sebastian Cavendish will keep the paper?"

Abby didn't want to raise her hopes. "I can't know what he'll do. I haven't even met the guy."

"You will soon enough. He'll be coming for the funeral."

"That might take a while to sort out."

"It's all organized. I typed up Dermot's detailed instructions a couple of years ago. He was very particular about the music he wanted played at his service and the guest list... He'd even written his own obituary." Faith sighed. "I hate talking about him in the past tense."

Abby sat up. "Had he been ill?"

"Ill? No, not that I know of. He'd been fit. Every day he used to walk around town stopping for a chat with people."

"Was that a habit with him or did he take up walking on doctor's orders?" Maybe the signs had been there but no one had noticed.

"He was a health fanatic and a vegetarian, which made him a bit of an oddity in these parts."

"What do you mean?"

"It's cattle country. You're staying at the pub. Just look at the menu. They serve slabs of meat. Although, the new chef they hired a while back made some changes to the menu."

"So, he didn't have a pre-existing condition," Abby mused. That meant there'd be a post mortem to determine cause of death. "Well, even healthy people have to meet their end."

"There's another call," Faith said, "Do you mind holding?" Faith didn't wait for her to answer.

Abby frowned and decided she had to be in shock and in need of someone to talk to. Shortly after she came back on the line.

"Sorry about that. It was Sebastian Cavendish. He's already been informed."

"How did he sound?" Abby asked, her reporter's curiosity kicking in.

Faith answered distractedly, "He always sounds brisk. As if he's ticking a task off a list but he was polite enough to ask about me. It's strange. I didn't actually expect to hear from him."

"Why not?"

"He's the type to delegate. He has scores of people to pick up the slack. Anyway, he wanted to know if Dermot had made funeral arrangements and he wants to go through some documents tomorrow."

"He's coming to Eden now?"

"Yes, although he said it might be a while before the body is released. I guess he wants to start getting the ball rolling." Faith moaned. "I'm never going to find a job as good as this one. And now I just heard myself.

Sorry, I'm still in shock."

"How about you meet me at the pub for a drink," Abby suggested.

"Yes, please."

"Give me half an hour to freshen up." Abby looked at her suitcase. She didn't see any point in unpacking now so she rummaged through it for a change of clothes but left everything else for later on.

Faith sat at the bar talking with Mitch Faydon. As Abby approached, she heard the drone of conversation drop down to a soft hum. Everyone's attention shifted to her.

"Faith, do you want to get a table? I wouldn't mind having a bite to eat. I skipped lunch, or maybe it was breakfast. Hard to say."

They moved over to a corner table next to a window overlooking the main street and the mountain ranges beyond.

"Word's spread like wild fire," Faith said, "Everyone knows."

"I guess they also know I'm the one who found Dermot Cavendish."

Faith nodded. "I didn't say anything. It must have been the neighbor."

"You'll have to point her out to me." Abby had a quick look at the menu and ordered a steak and fries.

"I'll have the same because if I don't, I'll end up stealing your chips," Faith said.

Abby smiled and made a mental note to switch from fries to chips. "There's something I've been meaning to ask. Is it normal for a detective to attend to an emergency call in a small town?" Abby remembered a couple of police officers arriving first and then the detective. She didn't know much about crime procedures but assumed a death would first have to be identified as suspicious before the big guns were called in.

"I don't think so. A police officer would be first on the scene."

"So what's the crime rate like in the area?" Abby asked.

"There are occasional speeding infringements and a bunch of local hooligans keep the police entertained. Anything else is unheard of."

"No murders?"

Faith gave a slow shake of her head. "Not in my lifetime. Why do you ask?"

"I'm wondering why a detective was called in on the scene."

Faith nodded. "Dermot was a prominent figure in the community. Also, he was a Cavendish. That's a big name in this country."

And beyond, Abby thought and rubbed her temple. "Did I imagine it, or did you say it might be a while before the body is released for burial?"

"That's what Sebastian Cavendish said."

"So, the death is suspicious," Abby mused.

Faith leaned forward. "What are you suggesting?"

"Nothing."

"You think someone had something to do with his death?"

Abby cleared her throat. "I didn't say that."

"But you suggested it. And not for the first time."

Abby shrugged. "I'm jet lagged and hungry."

Lowering her voice, Faith asked, "What if someone killed him? That would be huge news for us. Everyone will want to be kept up to date."

"Let's not jump to conclusions. He might have died of natural causes. And... If his grandson is determined to shut down the newspaper I doubt he'll postpone doing it just to give everyone a free update."

Faith sighed and looked out the window.

"Is it true?" Mitch Faydon set a basket of bread on the table.

Abby looked up and smiled, but before she could say anything, Faith jumped in and said, "Yes, it's true. The earth is round."

Mitch gave Faith a knowing smile and turned to Abby. "Let me guess, you've been asked not to say anything." He shrugged and arranged the cutlery on the table. "Here's a newsflash for you. The cat's already out of the bag."

"Is that what everyone here is talking about?" Abby asked innocently.

He shrugged. "Mostly, but they're also curious about you."

Abby made an open hand gesture. "I'm an open book."

Mitch flashed her a brilliant smile. "You also happen to be the person who found Dermot. How can we be sure he was already dead when you found him?"

Abby curved her eyebrows. "You're kidding."

The edge of his lip lifted. "We don't know anything about you."

"Mitch has a point," Faith piped in.

Abby sat back and folded her arms. "And yet, the detective I spoke with didn't say anything about not leaving town."

"Did he get your contact details?" Mitch asked.

He had.

"Does he know where you're staying?"

Abby bit the edge of her lip and nodded.

"What's his name?"

"Detective Inspector Ryan."

Mitch chortled. "Joshua."

"He's a local?" Abby asked.

Mitch nodded. "He's a fox. He wouldn't give anything away. I hate playing poker with him. And he has a way of getting people on side."

He'd given her coffee... As a way to gain her trust? "What are you suggesting?"

"Only that if there's anything suspicious about

Dermot's death, Joshua will get to the bottom of it. Slow and steady. I'd watch out for him, he tends to wear down his prey. And if you're thinking of making a run for it, be warned, there's only one main road out of town. He'll have someone watching it. At this point, your only chance will be to head for the hills... on foot, and then cut across country. If you're fit, you might make it to the next town, but I'd advise against that since by then, Joshua would have put an alert out on you."

"An alert?" Abby's head spun. "Why are you telling me this?"

Mitch Faydon grinned. "Apart from the news about Dermot, it's been an unusually slow day. In fact, this entire year has been slow."

Abby's voice filled with disbelief. "And you're taking your boredom out on me?"

"I just thought I'd warn you about Joshua." Mitch Faydon gave her a bright smile. "It's all part of our customer service."

Was he serious? And had Detective Joshua Ryan already started working on lowering her defenses by giving her the best coffee she'd had in a long while? "I stand warned," Abby said, getting into the spirit of it. When in Rome... do as the natives do, even if it meant walking on the wild side of loony. She took a sip of water. "When was the last time you saw Dermot alive or dead?" she asked Mitch.

He laughed. "Trick question. I like you."

Faith cupped her chin in her hand. "You didn't answer Abby's question."

"Do I look like a killer to you?"

Faith shrugged. "I've never met one."

"Well, I'm in the clear. Dermot came in yesterday... mid-afternoon. He caught up with a couple of his old friends."

"How does that put you in the clear?" Faith asked. "He was killed today."

"How do you know that?" Mitch asked. "Just because Abby found him soon after she arrived in Eden doesn't mean he died this morning."

Abby shook her head. "Did you talk to him yesterday?"

"I asked how he was doing, as you do. He talked a bit about a snoopy reporter coming to work for him and how he wished he'd done a more thorough job of checking her references because, for all he knew, he might have hired a serial killer." His eyes twinkled with amusement.

Abby gave him a brisk smile. "Were you on good terms with him?"

"Meaning... did I have a reason to want him dead? The police will have a hard time finding anyone who disliked Dermot."

Their conversation suddenly struck her as odd. What if Dermot hadn't died of natural causes? She'd been the first on the scene and the one to raise the alarm. Would she become a suspect? And if so, how would she prove her innocence? Abby visibly shivered. "Joking aside, I worked a murder trial once and it put me off for life."

"Nothing like this has ever happened in these parts," Mitch said, "It's only been a few hours and it's all anyone can talk about. If the cause of death turns out to be something other than natural causes, the pub's in for a busy time. Everyone will come into town to get updates."

"Let's hope it doesn't come to that," Faith said. "It'll mean there's a killer among us. Someone we know. Someone we trust. Maybe someone we don't think twice about letting inside our home or..." her voice rose slightly, "someone who pours our beer every day."

Abby looked around. "I was looking forward to living and working in a quiet little town. I guess that's not going to happen now."

Chapter Four

"Ready to order?" the waitress asked.

Abby had to force herself to focus. She'd managed to get some sleep, but not nearly enough to clear the cobwebs from her mind. She didn't think she'd ever read such an unusual and extensive menu. "I'm after a cup of coffee," she ventured. She'd woken up in the middle of the night and had called her mom to let her know she'd arrived safe and sound. The conversation had been hard to keep up with as she'd dozed off several times. Waking up that morning, her brain had fixed on the immediate need for a shot of caffeine, specifically, one from Joyce's Café.

"You sound overwhelmed."

And now she felt it. Thoroughly. Good manners fell by the wayside as she gave the server a head to toe sweep. Audrey Hepburn came to mind. Dressed in an outfit straight out of a fifties movie, her bright red lips lifted in a knowing smile.

"You're the new reporter."

Abby nodded and introduced herself.

"I'm Joyce Breeland. The owner." She tilted her head. "Did my menu confuse you?"

"It actually mesmerized me." Abby gazed down at the menu. "The Marcel Proust. The Midnight Express with or without a swagger?"

"They're the coffees for serious drinkers and yes, they will help you connect the dots."

That made sense. The French author, Marcel Proust, had been a night owl with an addiction for coffee. "And the swagger?" Abby asked.

"That's a dash of Brandy or Cognac. It's popular in winter and late evenings."

"I'll... I'll have The Midnight Express without the swagger. And I see you don't have egg white omelets. Any chance I might get one?" Abby looked up in time to see Joyce Breeland purse her lips. Had she hit a raw nerve?

"We don't do compromises," Joyce Breeland said, her tone polite yet firm. "Either you have eggs or you don't."

"I guess you feel strongly about that."

Joyce Breeland gave a small shrug. "Hannah at the pub does a great egg white omelet."

Abby tried to hide her surprise. She was used to a

less unique style of service. "Is there, by any chance, a story behind all this?"

Joyce's gaze danced around the café. "It's a small town. We tend to create our own entertainment so I'm going with, yes... there's a story. The one about the eggs probably started with Mitch—"

"Mitch Faydon, from the pub?"

"Yes. We don't always see eye to eye."

"So, there's an ongoing dispute about egg white omelets."

Joyce's eyes sparkled with amusement. "Not as such, and nothing is ever really serious."

"I see." Abby brushed her hand across her face. Maybe she had stepped into an episode of the Twilight Zone or she'd fallen through a rabbit hole. "Out of curiosity, do you know anything about the Lamington wars?"

"Oh yes, and it's not a war. It's just a saga that's been going on for ages. Why do you ask?"

"I'm... I was supposed to do a feature on it. To tell you the truth, I haven't actually had time to do any research. What exactly are Lamingtons?"

"There's a picture on page five." Joyce flicked through the menu and found the page for her. "They're a quintessential Australian cake, made from squares of sponge cake coated in an outer layer of chocolate sauce and rolled in desiccated coconut. The ongoing dispute is about variety. Some say you should only use strawberry jam for the filling, others are more liberal minded and enjoy experimenting."

"Where do you stand?"

Joyce gave her a small smile. "I'm neutral. I can't afford to express opinions that will alienate my customers."

And yet, she appeared to feel strongly about the egg white omelet... and the more Abby thought about it, the more she wanted one, but her need for coffee took precedence. She didn't dare risk being asked to leave Joyce's Café.

"I'll have a couple of Sunny Side Up Eggs and some toast, thanks." Her health kick could wait another day.

"Great choice."

Joyce Breeland didn't move away. Instead, she handed the order to another waitress. "I hear you're the one who found Dermot."

Did everyone know? "News travels fast."

Joyce sighed. "He came in here every morning for a cup of tea. This was his favorite table." Joyce ran her hand along the back of the chair. "It's going to take a long while to get used to not seeing him around town."

"Would you like to join me?" Abby asked. She wasn't surprised to find Joyce didn't need to be asked twice.

Joyce settled down opposite her. "I was about to take my break. I usually sit at that corner table and flick through my magazines."

But in times of loss, Abby thought, most people

avoided being alone and looked for company to share anecdotes and reminisce.

"Everyone knew him," Joyce continued.

"I'm surprised he chose to live here." Abby shrugged. "I mean, he is... was a Cavendish."

"He wouldn't have it any other way. Even when he was running the big newspaper in the city, he preferred to delegate and spend most of his time here."

Abby tried to remember what she'd read about him. He'd been a widower for a number of years and had never remarried.

"In fact, he liked it so much here," Joyce continued, "He chose to live in town instead of at the big house."

"The big house?"

"The Cavendish family owns a huge house in the area, Castle Lodge, up in the hills."

"We are in the hills."

"Further up. It's massive and not the sort of house you'd expect to find around here. Dermot's great-grandfather brought in an architect from Europe and most of the fixtures and fittings were imported. I think they even imported the grand staircase."

"But he didn't live there."

"No, he preferred his cottage in town. Castle Lodge has been closed for years, although they still have a caretaker and his wife. The family used to come up for weekends and longer stays in winter for the skiing. But that was before my time."

"I didn't see much of the inside of Dermot's house but I noticed he had a vast collection of books."

Joyce smiled. "Dermot loved to read. He was a passionate collector and loved to talk about books."

Belatedly, Abby wished she'd paid more attention to his bookshelves. She gazed out the window and wondered what might have been. The brief phone conversations she'd had with Dermot had been informal enough to come across as friendly.

"Do you know what's going to happen to the Gazette?" Joyce asked.

"I wish. I've come a long way and I'd hate to turn back now. From what I'm told, Dermot's grandson is not likely to be interested in keeping the newspaper going."

"Worse comes to worst, we'll figure something out."

Abby frowned. "What do you mean?"

"Someone could come along and buy it. We need a local newspaper."

"Not really. At the risk of doing myself out of a job, someone could set up a blog online."

"We already have one of those. Set up by someone who calls herself the *Eden Bloggess*."

"You don't sound happy about it."

"It's anonymous and I'm not comfortable having someone secretly hovering around and eavesdropping on conversations. It makes me self-conscious."

Abby couldn't help smiling. After only a few minutes, she picked up on Joyce Breeland's idiosyncrasy. When she spoke, she sounded serious, but her smile wasn't far behind.

"So what are your long-term plans?" Joyce asked, "Are you going to live in the pub?"

"For the time being, at least. The room's comfortable enough and I don't think I have a choice. I'm told there aren't any rentals available in the area."

"We'll help you figure something out."

We? Abby felt strangely comforted. As the new person in town, she hadn't expected to fit in straight-away. Smiling, she looked up just as Detective Joshua Ryan walked into the café. The detective placed an order at the counter, turned around and leaned against it. He stood there a moment looking at his cell phone. When he looked up, their gazes met. Recognition came fast. He pushed off the counter and approached her table. At the same time, Joyce rose to her feet.

"Nice meeting you but I have to get back to work. The rush hour is about to hit." Joyce gave the detective a nod and moved away.

"Mind if I join you?" the detective asked.

"Go for it." Abby's breakfast arrived in time to distract her from paying too much attention to the detective's easy smile and broad shoulders.

"Go ahead. Don't wait for me," he said.

Abby took a sip of her coffee and smiled. If she stayed on, she would definitely become a regular at Joyce's Café. "So, how's the investigation going?"

"What makes you think there is one?"

Abby shrugged. "I hear Dermot Cavendish didn't have a pre-existing condition. So going by what you said, I assume there's going to be an autopsy. I know that doesn't necessarily mean there's reason to suspect foul play, but…"

"You're a reporter," he said, "And you're getting a whiff of something worth pursuing."

Was she? "Maybe I'm just as curious as the next person. Everyone I've spoken with had only positive things to say about Dermot. Who would want to kill him and why?"

"Sometimes people who are in excellent health simply die of natural causes. Let's not assume—" he broke off and looked around him.

Abby smiled. "Yes, everyone's hanging on your every word." The buzz of conversation had actually died down when he'd joined her.

He leaned forward and lowered his voice. "I suppose you'll be meeting with Sebastian Cavendish today."

"I doubt it. He'll probably have other priorities to take care of." She too had some priorities to deal with. Her thinking had been somewhat skewered by the change in time zones, jet lag, and finding a dead body, but now...

No time like the present to engage her brain and try to come up with a backup plan. If the newspaper job fell through, as it was most likely to do, she'd have to hunt around for something else to keep her busy for a while and then start making plans to head back home. She

SONIA PARIN

took a sip of coffee but that left a bitter taste in her mouth. Nothing to do with the coffee, Abby thought. She simply couldn't go home again...

"Sebastian Cavendish will definitely want to meet with you to talk over what you saw."

Abby tilted her head. "And you know that because..."

"He asked for details and I gave them to him."

"I hope you also assured him I had nothing to do with his grandfather's death."

The detective held her gaze long enough to make her shift slightly in her chair. What had Mitch Faydon said? Josh knew how to wear down his prey. But she wasn't running and, she wasn't guilty. Abby straightened.

"Have you remembered any new details?" he asked. "Something you might have seen but not noticed at the time."

She shook her head and looked down at her cell phone to read a text that came through. Abby smiled.

"Good news?"

"It's about the stray I picked up yesterday. He's ready to be collected..."

Chapter Five

"I'll give you the good news first. There's nothing seriously wrong with Doyle," the vet's assistant said, "He's been roughing it for a while, but he'll be fine once he starts feeding regularly."

Doyle.

So, he had a name. That meant he had an owner. Abby gave him a scratch under the chin. "And the rest?"

Katherine sighed. "His owner passed away a month ago and there's no next of kin. I guess that's why no one noticed Doyle missing. We traced the details to another clinic in the next town."

A month alone? Abby cupped his face and looked into his large brown eyes. "Is there an adoption service here?" She didn't want to think about any other option.

Katherine shook her head. "We could put up a notice."

"What sort of breed is he?"

Katherine smiled. "Pure bred mutt."

"He looks smart. Do you think someone around here would like him?"

The vet's assistant gave a slow shake of her head. "Farmers tend to favor Blue Heelers, they're used as cattle dogs. I don't fancy his chances." Katherine hesitated. "And... we don't really have the space to keep him at the moment."

"What about temporary foster care?"

Katherine gave Doyle a light pat. "I'd take him in myself but I already have five dogs and a cat at home."

Doyle huffed out a breath and slumped his head on his paws. Abby swung away and gazed out the window. "Surely someone would love to have him. He's so placid. He'd be a great companion."

"He's probably still grieving. Otherwise, he should be more active. Anyone taking him on would have to make sure he got his daily exercise. He doesn't look like a couch potato. How about you? You two seem to get along well."

A dog? She didn't know the first thing about looking after a dog. Her mom had been allergic to dog and cat hair so Abby had grown up in a pet free household and had always been the only kid in the block without a pet. When she'd moved to the city for work, she'd lived in a small apartment and hadn't given the idea of adopting a pet any thought.

Abby shook her head. "Oh... no. I couldn't. I mean, I can't. I'm staying at the pub."

"So? Mitch won't mind. Before his sister Eddie moved out of the pub, she had a dog." Katherine frowned. "The only one you might have to worry about is Markus. He's the eldest Faydon brother. Matthew is the middle brother, but he's on vacation at the moment. My advice would be to steer clear of Markus and you should be fine."

The grumpy one, Abby thought...

"You realize this could get us both into trouble?"

Doyle whimpered.

"You'll have to do better than that. We need to fly under the radar." Holding Doyle in one arm and the bag of goodies she'd purchased at the vet in the other, Abby checked the street for traffic, but only out of habit since there weren't that many cars driving along the side street.

"The trick here is to pretend all is well. I know I should come clean and tell Mitch Faydon about you, but I'm going to try a different tactic, at least until I find out how he'll feel about having you stay with me. Needs must. You understand that. I know I'm taking a huge risk and probably an unnecessary one, but I'm sure once I present him with a fait accompli, he'll be more likely to go with the flow."

She peered in through the window and saw Mitch pouring a beer and chatting with a customer. When she saw him turn away, she scooped in a breath and strode into the pub, making a beeline for the stairs.

"Nothing to it," Abby whispered, "I bought enough food for a couple of days. You understand, I couldn't haul a larger bag, but there's more food coming. You don't need to worry about that anymore."

When she reached her room, she realized the absurdity of her plan. "Mitch looks like a reasonable guy." But what about his other brother, Markus Faydon?

She set Doyle down and got busy unpacking the water and food bowls. Even though Doyle had been cleaned up, she still couldn't make out his breed. "There must be something else other than pure bred mutt in you. In fact, I wouldn't be surprised if there's some pedigree blood in there somewhere."

Doyle appeared to roll his eyes.

"It's okay if there isn't. I like you just as you are." At the sound of a knock at the door she stilled and prayed Doyle wasn't the type to announce visitors with a bark.

Easing the door open, she peered out. Mitch! "Yes?"

"Sebastian Cavendish is downstairs asking for you."

Already? He must have just arrived in town, Abby thought. "Thanks. I'll... I'll be down in a minute."

"Is everything okay in there?"

She nodded. "Why do you ask?"

Mitch looked over her shoulder and then back at her, his look a mixture of amusement and concern. "There's something in the air. We're all asking all sorts of questions now. Almost as if no one trusts anyone."

Abby had no idea what to say to that, other than... "That makes sense." When he didn't move, she decided to ease the door shut saying, "I'll be down in a sec."

She closed the door and pressed her ear against it, trying to hear his receding steps but suddenly all she could hear was her own breathing and thumping heart.

When she turned, she saw Doyle peering from behind the couch.

"I think he's gone," she whispered. "I'll set up your water and food and then I'm going to have to trust you'll be quiet while I'm gone."

Sebastian Cavendish made a beeline for Abby.

Faith O'Keefe had been spot-on when she'd described his manner as brisk. Abby barely managed to offer her condolences when he ushered her to a corner table.

A head taller than everyone else in the bar, he was an imposing man and quite handsome, with hair the color of dark chocolate, and the type of square jaw she'd only ever seen on male models advertising expensive suits. He appeared to have an easy manner. For some reason, Abby had expected him to be abrupt and formal.

She tried to make small talk. "How was your drive here?"

"I flew in," he said, his tone matter of fact. "Are you up to talking?" he asked.

The question caught her off guard. Sure, he had an easy manner but she'd imagined someone of his caliber would want to cut to the chase. Then she realized he was really only being courteous and would actually expect her to talk, regardless of how she felt.

"I told the police everything I know." And she knew the detective had filled Sebastian in.

"I know it's only been a day and you're probably still in shock, but has anything else come to mind?"

Abby opened her mouth to say no, only to wonder if Sebastian knew something she didn't. Were the post mortem results in? Had Dermot's death now become a murder investigation? She'd already jumped to the conclusion. In her mind, Dermot had been killed.

"I just received a call from the police," he said, almost as if he'd read her mind. "The pathology tests confirmed the presence of cyanide. The levels were toxic enough to act quickly."

Abby frowned and tried to remember what she knew about post mortem tests. "That was quick work. How did they know to look for it? Cyanide is not part of the usual drug tests." She couldn't remember if she'd learned that through some of the research she'd done for that one and only murder trial she'd reported years before or if she'd picked it up on TV.

Sebastian leaned in. "You're right. I know you've

only just arrived in the country so you might not know this. There's been a spate of deaths..."

"I heard the reports during my drive over but I don't remember poison being mentioned as the cause of death."

"It's all I've been thinking about," he nodded. "Those deaths have a common factor linking them. They were unexpected. The victims had been in good health and so there's nothing immediately suspicious to raise the alarm. When I heard about Dermot's sudden death I knew there would be a post mortem performed. It's standard practice here when someone dies in their home unexpectedly. So I made a few phone calls. The examiner looking into the other deaths hadn't been looking for toxins. Not yet, anyway. He was working on a process of elimination."

Of course, being in the newspaper business, he had tapped into his instincts, and being the owner of the newspaper meant he had a lot of open doors at his disposal.

"If the examiner's investigations had continued at the normal pace," he added almost as if he felt compelled to spell it out for her, "It would have taken some time before he considered poison, if at all. Dermot hadn't been ill so it was natural for me to become suspicious. Anyone will tell you he didn't have any enemies and I'd be inclined to agree. But we don't always know everything. So, I specifically requested the examiner step up the investigation to include extreme causes such as poison."

Abby tucked her hair back. "Do you have any other suspicions?"

"The type that might lead to finger pointing?"

Abby frowned. Her jet lagged, sluggish brain had been about to form the same thought.

He shook his head. "You'd think Dermot would have made a few enemies along the way, but my grandfather had been universally admired."

"Yet someone thought he deserved a death by poison." Abby sat back and studied him for a moment. "Are you a naturally suspicious person?"

He looked surprised by her question. "I'm in the news business."

Abby tried not to shrink back in her chair. "About these other deaths... Is someone going around poisoning people?"

"If the police have linked the deaths, they're not letting on. I'm willing to bet anything they'll soon have proof the other deaths were also caused by poison."

"Any idea how it was ingested?"

Sebastian held her gaze. "The tea."

The teapot had been in plain sight with no effort made to hide it.

"How do you feel about canvassing the area?" he asked, "I trust the police to do their job, but it wouldn't hurt to have someone else asking questions."

"I'm not a crime reporter."

"You're a reporter. You know how to get answers. You also have the advantage of being new in town. People are naturally curious about you and will open up."

Had he just given her an assignment? "According to rumors, you wanted to close the newspaper."

"What else have you heard?"

"That during your last visit, you and your grandfather argued."

He gave an easy shrug. "We always argued. Every time we met, in fact, but that doesn't mean I killed him."

She frowned. "Why did you assume I'd suspect you?"

"Isn't that what you were leading to?"

Yes, but... "So he wasn't a major stakeholder in your newspaper?" Abby mused.

Sebastian chuckled. "Even if he had been, do you think I would kill my own grandfather just to get my hands on the business?"

"People have killed for less." Greed. Jealousy. Revenge.

He held her gaze for long moments before he answered. "The head of The Daily First has always been a major stock holder. The Cavendish family has a long-standing tradition of handing over the reins and stepping down."

"But Dermot didn't retire completely."

"The Eden Rise was the first newspaper established

by the Cavendish family," he explained. "Dermot had a soft spot for it. He couldn't help being sentimental. Also, the idea of retirement isn't in our blood."

"Are you sentimental enough to keep the Eden Rise running?"

"At a loss?" He gave her a brisk smile.

"In honor of your grandfather and everything he stood for." Abby had no idea what that might be. However, she had no trouble imagining Dermot had cared enough about the community to offer the newspaper for free.

"I suppose this is your way of asking if you still have a job."

It was Abby's turn to smile. She looked around the pub. "I'm not just thinking about myself. This is a small town. Closing the newspaper would have a significant and lasting impact on the locals."

"On the locals but not on the local economy."

Abby knew Faith would beg to differ. "Like I said, it's a small town. If one person loses their job, it creates ripples." Abby tilted her head and gave him a pensive look. "Aren't you worried about the bad publicity?"

He chuckled. "Heartless newspaper mogul denies small town of its gossip vine? It's the sort of news a rival newspaper would relish running."

Abby hoped he wouldn't like that and would do everything in his power to make sure it didn't happen.

"I'm actually surprised you haven't used this opportunity to apply for a job with The Daily First."

Why hadn't she? "I guess I have my heart set on spending the next twelve months living here," she surprised herself by saying.

"What's the incentive? This is hardly the place to establish a career."

At first, it had simply been about getting a job, but then... she'd wanted to put distance between herself and her previous life. That, Abby decided, was something he didn't need to know about. "I'm thinking of it as a working vacation. Or, at least, I had been." Her contract had been with Dermot. Now that he was gone, so was the job, especially if Sebastian Cavendish decided to shut the newspaper down. "Any chance you might sell The Eden Rise as a going concern?"

"It wouldn't be worth my while."

At least she'd asked.

"But I haven't actually said anything about closing it."

Abby instantly perked up.

He checked his watch and picked up the menu. "I assume you haven't had lunch?"

She hadn't thought about it. In fact, her appetite remained on a different time zone. "I'm happy to nibble on something."

"Good. It'll give us a chance to talk about investigating Dermot's murder. More so now that you seem satisfied of my innocence."

"Did I actually say I was?"

Chapter Six

"Who's this little guy?" Faith asked as she gave Doyle a scratch behind his ear.

Seeing Doyle lapping up the attention, Abby smiled. "I found him by the side of the road. Doyle's an orphan." Abby looked over her shoulder, much as she'd been doing since leaving the pub with Doyle curled up in her arms. "Out of curiosity, how do you think Mitch Faydon feels about dogs?"

"Mitch would be okay. His brother, Markus... I'm not so sure about." Faith chortled. "Did you sneak him into the pub?"

"I'm still jet lagged and not thinking clearly... therefore, I'm not entirely responsible for my actions. That's my excuse and I'm sticking to it." Abby looked out the window at a pickup truck parked at the curb. "I've noticed a few people going into the pub and leaving their dogs in their trucks. I guess that means the pub's not pet friendly."

"For starters, they're not pets. They're working cattle dogs," Faith explained. "And, generally, you can't take animals inside places that serve food."

"Help me out. I'm looking for a way around this dilemma. I hear Mitch's sister had a dog while she was living at the pub."

"Are you a worrier?" Faith asked.

Abby sighed. "I guess I'm coming across as one, so there's no point in denying it."

"I should talk. I spent the morning hunting down boxes to pack things in."

"Why?"

"Sebastian will want everything sorted out before he leaves. I managed to get started packing some of the archival material. A few months back I catalogued everything so it'll now be a matter of sending feelers out to see if any libraries are interested in acquiring some of it."

"You're obviously too efficient for your own good, but aren't you jumping the gun? Sebastian hasn't said anything yet."

"I'm trying to be realistic. Dermot didn't really need me working here. He could have left the front door open day and night and no one would have taken anything. Even if Sebastian keeps the newspaper going, he's going to realize I'm superfluous, cutthroat newspaper mogul that he is."

"You need to change that attitude. If Sebastian walks in right now, that's the last thing you should be saying. You serve a purpose. What if someone calls with a story? There has to be someone here to answer the phone and be the face of the Eden Rise Gazette."

Faith leaned in and asked, "Do you know something I don't?"

Abby shrugged. "I met with Sebastian at lunch and he didn't actually say anything about shutting down the newspaper. That has to mean something. I think we should play it by ear. Cheer up. There's no harm in hoping."

"Mitch's grandmother would say to keep a happy thought and the rest will follow."

"Sounds like a plan to me."

Faith still didn't look convinced. She bit the edge of her lip. "Dermot had the wages set up for automatic payment. Basically, that means we're covered for a year."

"There you go. That's good news. We can even use that to convince Sebastian to keep the paper running." A year would be long enough for Abby to figure out if this town would be a good fit for her. But it was too early to start thinking about long-term plans. When she'd hopped on that plane, she'd only been focused on putting some distance between herself and everything that had gone wrong in her life.

Another thought wove in. Sebastian had been right in saying this small-town newspaper was hardly the place for someone trying to establish themselves. At some point, she'd need to set some goals. "If he expects you to sort out the packing, then I don't see anyone cracking a whip. In your place, I'd drag my feet."

Faith smiled. "That's cunning."

Abby bit the edge of her lip. "I might actually have some leverage. Sebastian wants me to look into Dermot's death. He thinks a pair of fresh eyes might get some results. Personally, I think he's grasping at straws. But this might be his way of coping with his loss. You know, trying to do everything he can."

Faith instantly brightened. "You knew that when you came in and you waited until now to tell me?"

"Sorry."

"So, he's suspicious."

Abby nodded. "More so now that the post mortem report found toxins—"

"What? What type of toxin?"

"Cyanide."

"Dermot was poisoned?"

Reading Faith's expression, Abby said, "How? Why? I guess that's up to the police to find out."

"But you're going to do some digging of your own. Can I help?"

Abby worried her bottom lip. She'd expected to spend her first week getting to know everyone and reporting on the weekend's bake sale and... looking into the Lamington wars...

"I'm counting on you to help. Someone put cyanide

in Dermot's tea. Either they snuck it in or they actually sat down with Dermot." Had there been one cup or two? She remembered Detective Ryan saying the teapot had been lukewarm.

"That means..." Faith's mouth gaped open, her eyes widened with disbelief. "Someone he knew killed him? Someone we know?"

Why would she jump to that conclusion? "Yes, I suppose so. Quite possibly. Who knows? Maybe."

"But... But..." Faith leaned forward and whispered, "One of us?"

"The police have to be thinking about it. They've most likely started questioning locals and will then widen their net. I'll need a list of people who were close to Dermot and anyone you can think of who had anything to do with him."

"That'll be the entire town," Faith mused.

Over two thousand people.

"I know everyone thought highly of him, but can you think of someone who might have had a disagreement with him or maybe held a grudge?"

Grabbing a notepad, Faith sat back and tapped a pencil against her chin. "I can't even imagine it."

They had to start somewhere. "When I arrived yesterday I walked past here and saw you talking to a man in a suit."

Faith nodded. "Yes. Donovan Carmichael. He's in the antiquarian business. He travels around a lot looking for rare books. He actually buys and sells anything and everything. You know, antiques, but his main interest is in books."

While she'd only caught a brief glimpse of him, Abby had thought he'd been a businessman. The suit had looked good on him and that usually meant it came with an expensive price tag. "He must do well in the rare books and antiques business."

"I suspect there's old family money. I've come across a few of those types."

"What makes you think it's family money? This is a small town. Not exactly a hangout for millionaires."

Faith's eyes widened slightly. "There are plenty of wealthy people around these parts. Landowners and cattle breeders would be at the top of the pile. There are a few people who don't work. Off the top of my head, I can think of two locals who are independently wealthy. You wouldn't know it by looking at them. One of them leases his land for grazing. The other one just lives off investments. They both inherited money."

"And where did you get that information from?"

"It's sort of common knowledge. People talk."

Abby remembered Sebastian's look of amusement when she'd jokingly suggested he might have done away with his grandfather in order to inherit.

Even if she wanted to suspect him, she couldn't count money as a reason for murder. Being a newspaper mogul put him in the big leagues.

Okay... so Donovan Carmichael might be independently wealthy, but his passion for books and antiques made him a suspect. What if Dermot had what he wanted?

"Joyce mentioned yesterday Dermot collected books." Abby had assumed that meant he simply enjoyed being surrounded by books. "Are we talking about rare and expensive books?"

Faith nodded. "That's why Donovan was here. He's been chasing after a particular book and he seemed to think Dermot would know something about it." Faith dug around her desk drawer. "I've got his business card."

"Did he happen to mention a book title?"

"No, he was very cagey about it. I think it has to do with competition." Faith shrugged. "Not letting anyone else know what he's trying to get his hands on."

"It must be quite a book for him to keep the title a secret." Abby looked at the business card. It had a cell phone number but no address. "Did he stick around long enough to find out about Dermot?"

"He was only passing through. Donovan spends most of his time traveling around. This was his second trip to Eden in a week. Dermot wouldn't make the time to see him."

"Why is that?"

"He said he was too busy but..."

"What?"

"Donovan could get a bit pushy and Dermot didn't like that."

Abby remembered seeing Faith on the phone. "You didn't look happy."

Faith nodded. "After Donovan left, he called to pester me about making an appointment to see Dermot."

What if... "How did Donovan look to you when he first came in? Did he seem agitated? Was he maybe looking over his shoulder?"

Faith shrugged. "Nope. He has an obsessive nature and only talks about books. In fact, he doesn't even bother with the usual chit chat." She swiped the air with her hand. "He just cuts straight to the chase."

What if Donovan had swung by the newspaper after visiting Dermot's house as a way of covering his tracks? Abby turned away and faced the street. She tried to imagine Donovan arriving at the crack of dawn and paying Dermot a visit.

Why would he kill him?

He wanted something. A book Dermot either possessed or knew how to get. When Dermot refused to tell Donovan about it, the man lost his temper. Abby chortled. He lost his temper, asked for a cup of tea, poured the poison and...

Nice try, Abby. If Donovan had become enraged, he might have been driven to do something impulsive, inexplicable... violent.

"No," she said to herself, Donovan could not have poisoned Dermot.

"No to what?" Faith asked.

"I was just entertaining a silly thought. Never

mind." Although, it wouldn't hurt to find out what book Donovan was after and search Dermot's house for it. Surely Sebastian wouldn't mind her snooping around. "What about women? Dermot was a widower, but did he have someone special in his life?"

"Not that I can think of. Even if there had been someone, Dermot was old-fashioned. He would have been discreet. If it helps any, he had regular visitors over for afternoon tea."

"Anyone in particular?"

Faith got busy writing down a few names.

"What about the neighbor who saw me going into Dermot's house? Is she on the list?" Abby asked.

Faith shook her head. "Thelma Harrison. She lives across the street from Dermot's place. He didn't have any patience for her." Faith leaned in and whispered. "She has a reputation for spreading gossip."

Chapter Seven

"Okay. We have a list of names to work through. Now it's a matter of figuring out an angle. I can't go around knocking on people's doors and asking if they killed Dermot."

Doyle tilted his head.

"Yes, I'm talking to you, but only because there's no one around to hear me talking to a dog." She wondered if anyone would care. Being a new face in a small town, she could pretty much do as she pleased. Within reason, of course, since she wouldn't want to establish herself as the local nutcase. "Although, it could work in my favor. You know, as an ice-breaker."

A woman stepped out of a store and smiled, first at Doyle and then at her.

"She didn't seem to find it odd that I'm talking to you. On the other hand, if you happened to answer back..." Abby looked down at Doyle. "Are you likely to answer back?"

Doyle shook his head.

"No?"

When they came up to Joyce's Café, Abby peered inside. There were quite a few people in there. She saw Joyce standing behind the counter. Dressed in a black turtleneck sweater, black tights and black ballet shoes, she resembled Audrey Hepburn in the movie Wait Until Dark. When Abby caught her attention, she signaled for her to come out.

"Hi. What's up? Hey... who's this?" Joyce asked as she bent down to give Doyle a scratch. "I haven't seen him around."

"This is Doyle."

"It didn't take you long to settle in."

Abby drew out her list. "Do you recognize any of these names?" she asked and belatedly wondered why she hadn't asked if Joyce would be interested in adopting a dog. She looked down at Doyle just as he leaned against her leg.

"Yes. They're all customers," Joyce said.

"Are any of them in the café now?"

"Josephine. She's wearing the straw hat."

Abby peered inside and saw an elderly woman wearing a hat and reading a book.

"She comes in for tea and scones. After years of baking for a large family, she prefers to let others do the work for her."

"Anyone else?"

"Norma Reed. She usually only comes on Sundays. She meets her daughter and granddaughter for lunch, but she's here today. In fact, business has been good. Everyone is out and about wanting to hear some news about Dermot. Why are you asking about them?"

"I want to know if any of them spoke with Dermot the day he died."

Joyce smiled. "You should have started with that. June Laurie does his cleaning early in the morning. She goes in at eight and finishes at nine. That's been her routine for years. And, for the record, she already spoke with Joshua Ryan. She would have been the only person Dermot spoke with that day. I'm sure Faith told you he's been working from home." Joyce tapped her chin. "We should have noticed the fact we didn't see him. After June finished tidying up for him, he always went out for a brisk walk and catch-up with people."

So much for her Donovan Carmichael theory. The antiquarian could not have killed Dermot because the cleaning lady had been at the house.

"So, did the cleaning lady see anything unusual?" Abby asked.

"Are you suggesting June has been spreading gossip?"

Abby rolled her eyes. "I'm hoping she made a passing remark."

"Why would she?"

"Because she spoke with the police. That must

have made her suspicious. Also, talking with the police is not an everyday occurrence. Human nature being what it is, I assume she would have shared the experience."

Joyce nodded. "After she finished cleaning, she used to sit down for a cup of tea with Dermot, but she said he had been busy looking for something. She didn't know what. So, she left."

Had Dermot been looking for a book? "Does June live nearby?"

"On Edgar Street. Number twelve. But you won't find her at home now. She spends her afternoons at the library reading to kids."

"What about the others?"

"Liz Hamilton's a retired school teacher. She used to catch up with Dermot once a week. They used to pore over international newspapers. She came in earlier today."

"I guess none of them would have a reason to kill Dermot."

"None that I know of. But you never know. They might have been biding their time."

Abby frowned at her. "That's macabre."

Joyce gave a small shrug. "I've lived in this town my entire life. I can't help wondering... You think you know people, but we don't. Not really. I've been asking around and no one's seen anyone suspicious. I've watched enough movies to now wonder if they're all covering up for a local."

Abby tried to get her head around Joyce's way of thinking but gave up.

Joyce folded her arms. "At least I know I have an alibi."

"Do you?"

"My first customer came in at seven in the morning."

"That's an early start for you," Abby observed.

"I live above the café so I don't have far to travel."

"Can you give me a list of people who came in between nine and eleven?" That would take care of crossing a few people off her list. "If June Laurie finished cleaning at nine, then Dermot was killed after that. I arrived close to midday." She wondered if Detective Ryan had already reached that conclusion.

"Swing by later on. I'll ask the girls to help me put together a list in case I miss anyone."

"Any chance I might get a coffee to go?"

"Don't you want to come in?"

Abby gestured to Doyle. "Oh, and I want to head over to the library."

"Okay, but next time, feel free to come in."

"What about health inspectors?"

"Let me worry about that."

Abby stood across the road from the library. The cleaning lady, June Laurie, spent her afternoons there, reading to kids. Great community spirit, Abby thought as she checked her watch. She'd called the library to ask about their services. The librarian had been helpful, mentioning all schedules were posted outside the library. She was about to cross the street, when Detective Joshua Ryan pulled up and strode straight in.

Abby decided to wait until he left. What could he have been following up on? He'd already spoken with June Laurie. Surely, she'd been cleared of suspicion.

"Here he comes." Instinct told her to turn around and head in the opposite direction, but she decided to play the tourist card. After all, she'd only just arrived and was becoming acquainted with the town and all its services... and taking Doyle for a walk.

When Joshua spotted her, he waved.

"Just my luck. He's the friendly type." She picked Doyle up and made a mental note to get a leash for him.

"You're making yourself right at home," Joshua said and gave Doyle a scratch behind the ear.

At this rate, Doyle would end up with a bald patch. Everyone loved him, but no one wanted to take him. "This is the stray I told you I picked up."

"So, you're going to keep him?"

"I don't even know if I'm staying. It wouldn't be fair to him if we got attached and then I left." She smiled at him. "You seem to like him and he hasn't growled at you."

Joshua chuckled. "I work odd hours. It wouldn't be fair on a dog."

"Doyle's not that demanding. He only seems to need fresh water and food."

"And someone to carry him."

"Oh... this is just me being overcautious. I don't have a leash and I'm afraid he'll wander off."

"Give it a try. I bet he'll be happy to sit by your side."

Abby nodded but didn't set Doyle down. "What brings you to the library?"

"The obvious. Something to read."

"Really? What did you get?" She made a point of looking at his hands. His empty hands.

"I did my reading inside."

"You must be a speed reader, you only went inside a short while ago..." She bit her lip.

"Keeping tabs on me, Abby Maguire?"

She turned slightly and pointed at the store on the opposite street. "I was checking out the antique store... Brilliant Baubles..."

"Did you take Doyle inside?"

"No... We looked in through the window and the owner... Never mind."

"Let me guess. He scowled?"

"I thought I'd imagined it."

"Nope, you didn't. Bradford Mills doesn't like people coming into his store."

"Well, that's odd. What sort of business is he running?"

"The sort that gives him time to think without being interrupted."

"Why does the name sound familiar?"

"He used to be a reporter. He spent a number of years working in the US and UK. Then he inherited Brilliant Baubles and while he took time deciding what to do with the store, he fell in love with Joyce Breeland and decided to stay."

"Oh." It was the only response she could provide, as the thoughts whirling around her mind were too abstract. New to town. They meet. Probably clashed. Most likely, yes. Joyce and the scowling antique store owner? In love?

Joshua chuckled. "I think you were headed to the library and when you saw me, you decided to hang back."

"Why would I do that?"

"To avoid being questioned."

"I've told you everything I know."

"Including getting Joyce Breeland to work on a list of people who visited Dermot?" He laughed again. "I went to the café and found her working on the list."

"I guess this is where you warn me to stay away from the case."

"Are you sensible and likely to heed my advice?" He brushed his chin. "I suspect you're not."

Abby sighed. "You couldn't be more wrong. I'm a lifestyle reporter. Anything else makes me run a mile in the opposite direction."

"Bad experience?"

"Let's just say some people are not cut out for gruesome details."

"Or taking unnecessary risks," he remarked testily.

"You just saw me cross the street carrying Doyle because I didn't want to risk him being run over."

He looked up and down the empty street. "Right, because traffic is so heavy." He smiled. "Okay. I believe you're not going to snoop around and get yourself poisoned. Which reminds me. Are you a tea drinker?"

"I'm strictly a coffee drinker."

"Good. Keep it that way. And don't accept drinks from strangers, or anyone you've recently become acquainted with."

She hugged Doyle against her. "Right. Trust no one, except Joyce. I can't stop drinking her coffee now and I blame you."

When he laughed, his eyes lit up. "So, what's your theory about the case?" he asked.

"You want to compare notes with me?" Abby could not have sounded more surprised.

"If I had to guess, I'd say you were actually headed to the library to talk to June Laurie because you found out she's the cleaning lady in town and she might have noticed something, or someone."

"Now that you mention it, I'm told she always finished up at nine. That must have helped you determine the time of death."

"We put it at half an hour before you called for help."

"I called when I arrived and found him, and I'm sure Thelma Harrison can verify the time I arrived since she's the neighbor who saw me going in."

The detective crossed his arms. "Covering your tracks and making sure you have a solid alibi. Interesting."

"I'm only saying. Clearly you don't suspect me. Otherwise, I'm sure you would have hauled me in for questioning."

"Maybe we're still looking into you and waiting to receive some background information from Interpol."

Abby and Doyle huffed out a breath. "You could save me the trouble of going inside the library and tell me if June Laurie remembered anything else."

"Where's the fun in that. You might find out something I haven't been able to get out of her."

"A moment ago, you suggested I should keep out of your investigation. Are you now encouraging me to snoop around?"

"No. I'm not. However, I don't see the harm in you asking questions, but if you happen to walk into a perilous situation, I'd have to come down hard on you. By all means, have a chat with June. It won't hurt."

Because he didn't expect her to find anything new? What sort of reverse psychology was he trying out on her?

"What's that smile about?" he asked.

"I was just entertaining a few stray thoughts. Running through what I already know. June used to sit down to have a cup of tea with Dermot. Everyone knows that. What if she prepared the tea but, seeing how busy Dermot was, she left him to it? It would make a perfect alibi."

The detective appeared to think about it for a moment. "Are you suggesting she poisoned the tea and made up an excuse about Dermot being busy?"

"Isn't it strange that the neighbor, Thelma Harrison, saw me arriving but she didn't notice anyone else?" She waited for him to ask about motives. Luckily, he didn't.

He held her gaze for a moment and then looked over his shoulder toward the library.

Had she given the detective a lead? "Wait, there's more." She smiled. "What if the poisoned tea had been there all along?" Anyone who visited Dermot could have poisoned the tea leaves. She needed to find out if June Laurie had drunk some of the tea.

Chapter Eight

*C*yanide. "How on earth would I get my hands on it? Walk up to the drugstore counter and say... I'll take some Advil and... oh, yes... some cyanide, please."

"Can I help you?"

Abby stepped back. She'd been so lost in thought, she hadn't seen the sales clerk approaching her. "I'm... I'm new in town and getting acquainted with what's what and where."

She hadn't been able to catch up with June because she'd already left. So Abby had headed back to the pub but along the way, she'd been wondering how one went about procuring such a toxic poison. When she'd reached the drugstore, she'd stopped at the door. She really needed to get a leash for Doyle. Even if he didn't wander off, she'd feel better about leaving him outside.

Abby pointed at Doyle. "I'd love to come in and have a look around but I can't leave him outside."

The sales clerk looked fresh out of high school and possibly a little suspicious of someone acting strangely.

Before Abby could figure out a way to ask about the sale of poisons, the girl beat a hasty retreat saying, "If there's anything you need, just holler."

As Abby turned away, she caught sight of Joshua driving by. He waved to her and kept going. She didn't think she'd given him a real lead. Where would June Laurie get cyanide? A quick search online had been fruitless. Although...

"If I collect enough apple seeds and follow instructions, I might be able to extract enough cyanide to make someone sick. How about we find out if there's an apple orchard nearby?" Doyle didn't answer. In fact, he looked ready for a nap. "Come on. Let's go see if we can find you a leash." Although, with Joshua Ryan off chasing down his next suspect, the way was clear for her to have a chat with June Laurie. She lived near Dermot's place. Before she could decide if she should beat a path to her front door, she'd arrived at the vet's clinic.

"The one place in town where we can stroll in without any hassles."

Doyle whimpered slightly.

"Don't worry. We're only here to get a leash." Katherine was with a client so Abby had a look around the shelves. "See anything you like?" she asked Doyle.

"Do you expect him to answer?"

Abby turned. "Um... No. But there's always a first time. Hi, I'm Abby."

"I'm Pete Cummings, the vet." He stooped down. "And I remember this little guy. How's he doing?"

"I think he's still getting used to me."

Pete Cummings had an easy smile and the sort of hair that needed constant brushing back.

"You might want to try the little body harness. It'll sit comfortably on him without being restrictive." He took one off the shelf and tried it on for size.

"That looks good and Doyle doesn't seem to mind it. We'll take it. Oh, and we might try this little coat on too. I hear it gets cold around here in winter." She selected a red tartan coat and slipped it on. "Perfect." She watched Doyle exchange a look with Pete Cummings that spoke of male tolerance in the face of adversity. "Thanks, you've been very helpful." She turned away to pay for the items when it occurred to ask, "Is cyanide used in vet clinics?" And if so, did he have some handy? His stunned expression told her she should have eased into the question. "Sorry, I didn't introduce myself properly, I'm actually the new reporter at the Eden Rise Gazette and I'm researching an article I want to write."

Pete gave a cautious nod "Cyanide is used for animal pest control such as possums."

"How effective is it?"

"Animals are unconscious within a few minutes.

The poison works through their system quickly so it doesn't affect other predators."

"Does it work on people?"

He frowned. "Yes, but... the person would have to be willing. Cyanide has a strong flavor and you're talking about animal pest control products, so they come in pellets." His frown deepened. "Did you say you were writing an article?"

"I know, it sounds suspicious. I promise I'm not looking for ways to kill someone."

"Oh, my goodness..." a woman behind her exclaimed.

"I think you frightened Mrs. Bailey."

Abby turned and offered a small smile. "Maybe I should just pay for my purchases and get going. Thanks for your help."

She spent the next half hour walking around town, trying to get the lay of the land and maybe come up with some ideas about Dermot's death. Finally they came to a stop in what looked like a town square at the end of the main street. It had a playground at one end and some sort of memorial sculpture at the centre surrounded by a copse of trees.

"Every town has its hero," she murmured as she came up to a memorial to fallen soldiers. She read the plaque and, looking at the modern looking sculpture, tried to make sense of it. A mound of sharp edged rectangles formed a nest. A fisted hand emerged from within it, with another hand pointed at the sky palm up, its symbolism lost on her.

Doyle and Abby stood there looking at it, their heads tilting from one side to the other. "I guess this is open to interpretation. What do you think, Doyle? Personally, I like the color." She'd seen that blue-green tint on statues that had been exposed to the elements, but the sculpture was only a recent addition. "Trick of the trade?"

"Okay, Doyle. Here's the deal. After I sneak us in, you can have a nap while I get something to eat." Once again, she made it to her apartment undetected. Inside, she changed his drinking water. "Hey, you didn't touch your food. What's up with that? Not hungry?"

Doyle proved her wrong by nearly falling into his bowl and munching most of the food in one go.

"I'll see you soon. Try not to snore too loudly. Remember, you don't want to attract attention."

Downstairs, she found a table by a window and worked on a plan of action for the next day. In hindsight, she was glad she hadn't gone to June's house as that might have triggered alarm bells with the cleaning lady so soon after Joshua Ryan had gone in to talk with her for a second time.

"Getting an early start on dinner or are you just after a drink?" Mitch asked as he gave the table a brisk wipe.

"Some food, please."

"How's your day been? Caught the killer yet?"

"What makes you think..." she stopped and shook her head. "If news spreads like wild fire in this town, why is it no one knows who the killer is? Are you all covering up for one of your own?" She held her hand up. "I take it back."

"Glad to hear it. We're happy to joke around, but when it comes to something as serious as Dermot's death..." Something flickered in Mitch Faydon's eyes— a reminder that everyone had been touched by Dermot's death.

"It must be tough knowing one of your own might be responsible." She glanced through the menu. "Will I be happy with a burger?"

Mitch gave a small nod. "You'll probably want to write an article about it."

While she waited for her order, she got her cell phone out and researched cyanide.

"That's one mystery solved and... You learn something new every day," she murmured. She'd had no idea cyanide could be used to achieve the blue color on cast bronze sculptures.

Mitch set a glass in front of her. "Here's a drink on the house."

"Water?" She took a sip only to stop.

"Where's your trust?"

"Said the spider to the fly." Abby lifted the glass in a

salute and drank deeply. "Are there any artists in the area?"

"Bartholomew Carr," Mitch said. "He has a studio on the outskirts of town. Why do you ask?"

"Is he, by any chance, responsible for the sculpture in the town square?"

"As a matter of fact, yes. The memorial went up last year. Dermot organized an art competition to select the most appropriate piece."

"I guess that means Bartholomew won. Was he the popular choice?"

"Not mine or Dermot's. I mean... come on. Have you seen it?" Mitch chuckled. "This is a small town. You'd be hard pressed to find someone who's ever set foot inside an art gallery. Regular people, and yeah, that includes me, want to know what something means."

Abby made a mental note to chase this up.

"What's on your mind?"

"Cyanide is used to get the blue color on bronze sculptures." She gestured for him to lean down. "Cyanide was the killer's weapon of choice. You didn't hear that from me."

Mitch laughed. "So now you're going to suspect our local artist? I'd love to be a fly on the wall when you confront him about it."

"I'm going to have a chat with him. There's only so much information I can find online about cyanide. He might be able to help me."

"Good luck with that."

"I don't like the sound of your tone. Should I be worried?"

"He's a temperamental character," Mitch explained.

"That goes hand in hand with his profession so I guess I'll be fine." When her burger arrived, Abby sank her teeth into it and nearly fainted. "Oh, this is heavenly."

"Prime beef. Can't do any better. Although, our vegetarian burger is a big seller too. Not that anyone will actually own up to liking it."

Taking another bite, she entertained thoughts of staying on at the pub forever.

"How about a beer to wash it down?" Mitch suggested.

She managed a nod and went right back to enjoying her gourmet feast. As she wafted back down from her trip to cattle country heaven, she noticed the photographs covering the walls. She'd actually seen them the first day she'd arrived, but she hadn't stopped to take a closer look.

"A.C. Faydon. June 1830." The man in the photo wore a suit and sported a beard. Behind him, a sign read Grand Opening. The next photo showed three men and a woman standing in front of The Gloriana, all dressed in modern clothes. She recognized Mitch Faydon and guessed the others were his brothers and sister. The photo should have been in color. Instead, it looked like the 1830 sepia picture next to it.

As she continued to study the photos, conversation

wafted around her. A country tune played in the background. Customers came and went.

Abby guessed everyone in town would have similar images linking them to a distant past. Deep roots ran here. As a newcomer, she could only skim the surface but she would never really know how everyone really felt about what had happened.

She spent some time doing more research, which included looking up the artist, Bartholomew Carr. Another local with links to the town, she thought as she studied the photos on his blog. Taking note of his studio address, she finished her meal and decided to pay him a visit. But first she had to check on Doyle... and sneak him out of the apartment.

She found him snuggled up in a corner of the couch. "Should I be making up rules about you and the couch? I don't want to think you're taking advantage of me because you sense I know nothing about pet discipline."

He opened one eye and raised his brows at her.

"Are you suggesting we share? That depends. Do you shed?" She brushed her hand along the couch. "Yeah, you do. Okay, we'll compromise. I'll get a blanket but you must promise to stick to your side of the couch." She grabbed a jacket from her suitcase. As she turned, she noticed his food bowl was half full. "I told you there's plenty more food. No need to ration it. Come on, we're going for a drive. I'd like to make an inroad into my list of suspects, which now includes a new name." Doyle had a leisurely stretch and yawn and then hopped off the couch.

Along the way, she got a call from Sebastian Cavendish asking for a progress report.

"Nothing so far," Abby said. "I'm focusing on getting an idea of how people go about getting their hands on cyanide. Also, I wouldn't mind having a wander around Dermot's house."

"I'm staying there at the moment," Sebastian said. "Drop by tonight."

"Whatever you do, don't offer me anything to drink... or to eat. You're not off the hook yet." Abby didn't wait to hear the response from her prospective new employer. "Talk to you later. Another call's coming through." She checked the caller ID. "Faith. How are you holding up?"

"Puzzled you haven't contacted me with news," Faith complained.

"That's because I don't have anything yet. Hey, what can you tell me about Bartholomew Carr?"

"He's grumpy most of the time. Walks around with a perpetual scowl and a sneer."

"Is there anything I should know about him winning the commission for the memorial in the park?"

"Have you seen the sculpture?" Faith asked. "It's horrible and no one gets it. We would have preferred something abstract. That way, we could have justified not understanding it. You've got these two hands jutting out of a violent looking nest. What's that all about?"

Abby grimaced. "Knowing how touchy artists can be, I guess I'll be risking life and limb if I ask."

"If you want anything from him," Faith said, "I suggest you play it safe. Compliment his art first and then shoot from the hip."

"Does he have any admirers?"

"None that I can think of."

"So how did Bartholomew end up winning the commission?" Abby asked.

"You can blame the selection committee for making the unanimous decision. They came from the city."

"I'm surprised I'm not investigating Bartholomew's death. He doesn't sound like a popular guy."

Faith's tone lost all its chirpiness. "I'll let you form your own opinions."

"I think it's a bit late for that, I'm already biased. If you don't hear from me again, you'll know where to start looking."

"In your place, I wouldn't disconnect the call," Faith suggested. "You never know."

"That's okay. I've got Doyle with me." Right on cue, Doyle produced a gruff bark. "Good boy, Doyle."

Chapter Nine

*D*riving under the speed limit made her a sitting target. In the short drive out to Bartholomew's studio, Abby must have encountered every driver in the area speeding past her. "Where's the police when you need them?" She glanced out the driver's window in time to catch a series of hand gestures she had no way of interpreting without blurting out a few expletives.

"Have a nice day, buddy." She waved at the driver as he sped off.

Doyle shrunk into the corner of the passenger seat.

"What's the matter with you? Embarrassed to be seen with me? I can't help being a cautious driver. I'm not used to driving on the wrong side of the road. We share the same language, more or less, why can't we share the same road rules? Also, I'm trying to take in the pretty scenery." And there was plenty of it around.

Abby felt her shoulders ease down as she glanced at the houses in the distance surrounded by farmland and undulating hills with the mountains as a backdrop.

Doyle edged toward her and rested his chin on her lap.

"Don't worry. You can criticize me if you like. I won't hold it against you." To her surprise, Bartholomew had been allocated his own road sign. "Loathed and revered at the same time. It really doesn't make sense. What does that tell you about the good folk of Eden?" She patted Doyle on the rump. "Probably that they're willing to tolerate his idiosyncratic nature and artistic temperament because..." Nope, she couldn't think of a single reason why.

Turning into a tree-lined driveway, she brought her car to a stop, scooped Doyle up, and emerged from her car. "I'm going to set you down. Please stay by my side." She looked up and into a spacious garage that appeared to have been converted into a studio. A man sporting a long beard and scruffy jeans stood brushing his hand across his chin.

Narrowing her gaze, Abby saw that he stood in front of a sculpture. "This has to be a good sign. The man has an open studio. Clearly he doesn't mind visitors."

When he turned and faced her, Abby understood what Faith had meant about the perpetual scowl. "Fierce comes to mind." But he appeared to be receptive. Matching her steps, he met her half way.

When she introduced herself, he again surprised her

with a nod. Clearly, he didn't mind reporters. "I've heard a lot about your work." Time to butter up the local artist. "I'll be writing a face of the town series and thought it would be fantastic to kick it off with a piece about you." The artist didn't need any more encouragement to talk about himself. She ended up filling ten pages of notes to justify asking, "How did you feel about Dermot?"

Bartholomew's growl matched his scowl. Dermot's only crime had been to withhold all deference. He hadn't printed or expressed a single word of praise for the artist and that had been enough to set him on a warpath.

Unfortunately, Bartholomew had been all talk and no action. He could at least have trodden on Dermot's garden or thrown something through his window.

"So, you were..." Furious. Enraged. Seeing red. Abby bit the edge of her lip and smiled. "Disappointed by his lack of interest in your work."

"Don't get me wrong," he said, "My last show sold out but I didn't get a single review in the papers. I know Dermot Cavendish pulled strings to get me boycotted."

Abby gave herself top marks for patience, biding her time until she found another opening. When she did, she put everything she had into steering the conversation toward cyanide. "Do you use that in your sculptures?"

Halfway through explaining the process, he stopped. "Wait a minute. What's this about?"

Responding to Bartholomew's hard tone, Doyle

sprung to his feet in readiness for a brisk getaway. Smart dog.

"You think I killed him? Just because I use the stuff for my sculptures? Am I the only one under suspicion or are you going around pointing the finger at anyone who uses cyanide?"

"How did you know Dermot was poisoned?"

"It's a small town. Word spreads."

Abby remembered mentioning it to Mitch at the pub. Had someone overheard her? Despite Bartholomew nearly standing toe-to-toe with Abby, she stood her ground. "It's not exactly your run of the mill ingredient found in everyone's kitchen cupboard."

"Oh, yeah?" He looked her square in the eye. "So, you've questioned Richard Armstrong?"

"Who's he?"

"He owns the photography studio in town. And what about Annabelle Hugh?" He took a step toward her forcing her to take a retreating step. "She owns the jewelry store."

"And they both use cyanide?" Abby asked innocently.

He stabbed the space in front of him with an accusing finger. "You bet they do. It's also used for animal pest control. Look around you. How many farmers do you think store it in their sheds?"

Okay, this trip had become quite educational. She'd had no idea cyanide was also used in jewelry making and certain kinds of photography such as sepia toning.

However... She lifted her chin a notch. "Do they have any grievances against Dermot?"

The accusatory finger sprung out again. "Tread with care, lady."

Doyle surprised her by stepping forward and letting off a soft growl. It actually worked a treat, diffusing the situation. Bartholomew threw his head back and roared with laughter at Doyle's attempt to look threatening.

"You did very well back there, Doyle," Abby praised him as they drove off. "Out of curiosity, what would you have done if Bartholomew had become violent?"

Doyle lifted his chin.

"You have a secret weapon? Okay, I won't push you." Abby sighed. "You're probably thinking I'm not a very good reporter. To be fair to me, crime reporting is not my area of expertise. I'm more of a lifestyle reporter. It can be tough trying to get people to admit they've had help decorating their homes. Most will try to claim they've done it all on their own, but I tell you, once I sniff out a little white lie, I pursue it like the proverbial dog with a bone."

It hadn't all been a dismal failure. She now had two more names to add to her list of possible suspects... along with all the farmers in the area. However, she'd have to be more cunning when she approached her next person of interest. "I'll focus on my original assignment.

Pretend to do my face of the town series and somehow get people to talk about Dermot."

An image of Dermot filled her thoughts. Had he known his killer? Had they talked as he sipped his tea? The thought of a casual encounter with underlying intentions made her shiver.

Faith had put it into perspective expressing her fears about someone they knew being a killer. "I'm now thinking going out there to see Bartholomew could have ended badly for us."

Doyle sighed.

"Yeah, I'll know better next time."

By the time she returned to town, the sun had disappeared behind the mountains. "Let's swing by Dermot's house and check in with Sebastian. Not that I have anything to report. But at least I'll get a chance to have a look around the house. Who knows, it might refresh my memory."

Abby left her car at the pub and walked to Dermot's house. Halfway there, she wished she hadn't. Old-fashioned street-lamps lit the way, but the light cast a gloomy glow in the narrow cobbled streets.

As Abby strode along, she thought she caught sight of curtains shifting slightly. The feeling of being watched made the hair on the back of her head spring up.

Doyle trotted beside her, his gaze attentive.

"If you hear anything or see anyone, you'll let me know, won't you, Doyle?"

The enticing aroma of cooking greeted Abby at the door. Sebastian gestured for her to come in. Doyle surprised her with his exemplary social graces, staying by her side while any other dog might have gone wandering around.

"Expecting company?" she asked.

Sebastian nodded. "Yes. You. I hope you like pasta."

Noticing a light dusting of flour on his hands, she asked, "Are you going to impress me with home-made pasta?"

"It's one of my quirks. It relaxes me," he said.

"This is where I say you are full of surprises."

"You should reserve judgment until you've tried what I made. It's a recipe I picked up during my travels in Tuscany. The wine is from a local vineyard. It's quite robust and should go nicely with the meal." Sebastian showed her through to the kitchen where he got busy stirring a pot. "Any luck today?"

Abby settled on a stool and stole a few curious glances around. The kitchen looked wonderfully homey with a large collection of copper pots and ceramic containers with enticing promises of delicious cookies. Focusing her attention on Sebastian, she tried to gauge her response to him. Considering her recent experience with a male insect, she'd be surprised if her inner radar blipped. It didn't. Yes, she could appreciate Sebastian's centerfold good looks, but she didn't sense any response to it. Shaking her head, Abby caught him up on the leads she'd followed.

Sebastian set his wooden spoon down. "It's hard to imagine Dermot's cleaning lady poisoning him."

"But it's an interesting idea. She might have given him a full dose on the day or she could have poisoned him over time. It's only a theory and not really a viable one, now that I think about it. If she'd been giving him small doses, he would have shown signs of illness and everyone says he was in perfect health."

"She'd also need a motive," Sebastian said.

Abby shrugged. "Temporary insanity. Any one of the women in his life might have been trying to capture his attention."

"A woman scorned?" Sebastian laughed.

Abby watched him pour some wine into an elegant glass. "If you don't mind, I'll wait for you to take a sip first."

Smiling, Sebastian lifted his glass and took a drink. "Satisfied."

"I don't know... You might have an antidote." Abby tasted the wine. Smiling with appreciation, she created a mental list. Ten good reasons why she should stay on in this strange little town. Great coffee and wine headed the list right along with the locals, who were friendly and unusual. Even if the job fell through, she could find something else to keep her busy for the next twelve months.

She was about to ask if the police had given him an

update when his cell phone rang. Sebastian excused himself to take the call and she took the opportunity to have a wander around the house, starting with the sitting room where she'd found Dermot.

Abby noticed an entire bookcase full of first editions, but nothing over ten years old. Certainly nothing that would qualify as a collector's gold nugget. The next bookcase, however, looked more promising as she recognized a few titles and their dust jackets. First editions dating back to the 1960s.

Photos in elaborate picture frames were stacked on the mantelpiece. Faith would have to look at those to see if she could identify anyone. It would be interesting to see if any of the women on her list of people who regularly got together with Dermot appeared on the photos.

As the thought took shape in her mind, she stopped to look at a color photograph of Dermot and a couple of women sitting outside Joyce's Café. They were all looking at the camera, bright smiles on their faces. Studying the photo more closely, she noticed a woman sitting a couple of tables away from the group. Her eyes appeared to be glued on Dermot and her expression was anything but friendly.

"Hello, person of interest." Abby drew out her cell phone and took a few close-up shots of the photo thinking either Faith or Joyce could help her identify some of the people in it.

Overall, Abby had the impression of layers. Dermot enjoyed intellectual pursuits but the many photographs spread around his house were testaments to healthy relationships maintained and nurtured over time.

When Sebastian finished his phone call, he ushered her into the dining room. They spent the next couple of hours hashing over everything she had, playing around with ideas until they all seemed too ludicrous to consider.

"I went through his diary," Sebastian said as he reached out to a side table and retrieved a leather-bound book. "He kept meticulous notes of everyone he met. This is his most current one."

Abby nodded. "Faith mentioned he'd been working on his memoirs. I'd be interested to have a look through his notes."

"Feel free to look around. Everything is bound to be in his study. The police took his laptop, so you won't have access to that until they return it. But knowing Dermot, he would have kept a handwritten notebook. There's a whole bookcase of them."

"I still don't get how he could have drunk a cup full of cyanide without sensing something odd about it. From what I understand, it has a strong almond flavor. Surely he would have detected it." Abby sat back and looked up at the ceiling.

"What?"

"I just remembered something Joyce Breeland said. Not the exact comment but rather the tone. She'd sounded macabre. Maybe I need to start thinking like a killer. What if... what if someone held a gun to Dermot and forced him to drink the tea? There were no signs of a struggle. That could mean he was resigned to his fate. I imagine a killer leaving him no option. Talking him through the process, all the while waving a gun at him." Abby shivered.

"That's a vivid imagination, but I'm willing to go along with it." Sebastian brushed his hand across his chin. "Dermot was passionate about his tea and considered himself a connoisseur. You're right. He would have detected the difference in the taste."

She told him about her visit to the artist's studio.

"That sounds like a dangerous run-in. However, Bartholomew is all bark and no bite."

"I guess everyone puts up with him because he's an artist."

Sebastian shook his head. "He doesn't have any heirs. It's common knowledge he's left everything to the town. Part of the money goes to the maintenance of his house as an art gallery. The rest is supposed to go toward study grants and whatever relief the town deems suitable. We get a lot of bushfires in the area and every year there's someone in need."

A man with a big heart. "Hang on. Did Dermot leave a similar bequest?"

"He did, but I'm not about to suspect the entire town."

"How are the bequests handled?"

"There's a committee. Yes, Dermot sat on it. They're open to suggestions from anyone and, of course, if an individual is in need they're encouraged to apply for a grant."

It would be worth looking into. If someone had been rejected, they might feel disgruntled enough to take matters into their own hands.

As she helped him clear the table, she inspected the canisters of tea. Yes, Dermot had been quite a connoisseur, enjoying several varieties of tea. "Have the police checked these out?"

"They're still here, but that's not to say they haven't taken samples." He turned to her. "Coffee?"

"I think I'll pass. Thank you."

Chapter Ten

*T*he next day, Abby had an early start with her focus still glued on learning everything she could about cyanide. She left Doyle stretched out on the couch and went down for breakfast, her attention fixed on her cell phone as she entered the dining area.

"Table for one?"

Startled by the bear with a sore head growl, she looked up. "Hello."

The man hitched his hands on his hips.

"Markus!" someone called out to him. "Down boy. She's a guest."

Markus Faydon. The older brother... We meet at last, Abby thought and couldn't help shrinking back slightly. "I'm Abby."

He looked at her in silence and then leaned in. "You're hiding something."

"Lurch! Just show the guest through."

Abby peered around his head-taller-than-her frame and saw a redhead sitting at one of the tables with Mitch Faydon who waved to her saying, "He doesn't bite. Just shove past him."

To her surprise, Markus stepped aside and made a flourishing wave with his hand. Smiling, Abby took a tentative step toward a vacant table but Mitch called her over.

"Come join us. This is my sister, Eddie, and you've met Markus."

Abby smiled. "Hi. I feel as though I've been put through a test. Did I pass muster?"

"You did well," Eddie Faydon gave her a brisk nod. "So, you're the new reporter at the Gazette."

Abby couldn't help admiring Eddie's luscious locks. "Interim."

"We need a local paper. Sebastian wouldn't dare shut it down, and if it comes to that, we'll take up arms."

Abby picked up a menu. "Really? You feel that strongly about it?"

"We want to grow the town, not shrink it," Eddie explained. "The Gazette opened at the same time as the pub. It would be like losing a family member."

"Let Abby order her breakfast, Eddie." Mitch turned to her. "Any news about Dermot yet?"

"I'm sure the police are doing all they can." Abby waved her cell phone. "And, yes, I'm sticking my nose in."

"Don't mind us. Go ahead and research." Eddie leaned forward. "But you have to share."

"Okay." Abby scrolled along and found an article about a jeweler who'd been found dead in his apartment. Firefighters had arrived on the scene and had found a large amount of white powder spread across a countertop next to a can labeled cyanide.

Run for your life, Abby thought and was pleased to read the firefighters had backed out of the man's apartment and had called in the hazardous materials experts.

Scanning through the rest of the article, she stopped to read, "An accidental mixture of cyanide powder and water creates a deadly gas, like that used in the gas chamber." That raised questions and possibilities she hadn't considered.

She'd been happy to cross off the cleaning lady as a suspect, mostly because Dermot had not displayed any symptoms of illness before his death, but what if...

Abby tapped her finger on the cell phone and tried to picture June Laurie preparing the tea. Before leaving for the day, she dropped some cyanide powder into the teapot, walking away before the mixture produced a deadly gas, which had then killed Dermot because June had positioned the teapot next to him.

Dismissing the idea as too far-fetched and remembering Dermot had ingested the poison, she continued reading only to stop again. He could have poured himself a cup of tea. By then, the deadly gas produced by the teapot might have started taking effect and

Dermot could have drunk his tea without really noticing the odd flavor. But what possible motive could June Laurie have?

"How do you get your hands on cyanide?" Eddie Faydon asked.

"That's what I've been asking myself. Here we go, potassium cyanide and sodium cyanide are used for cleaning jewelry and are legal to buy for home-based businesses." Scrolling through she found a science lab supplier and was surprised to find it could be purchased for less than fifty dollars.

"Yes, but... Can it kill you?" Eddie asked as Markus approached. "I mean, how would one know how much to use?"

"I guess any amount can make you ill. Use enough, and death can occur in 2-6 hours. It could be mixed with sugar or salt..."

Markus lifted an eyebrow. "Time to step up security at the pub." He gave Abby a pointed look. "What do we know about you?"

They all looked at her.

"I'm..." Abby straightened. "The police are currently running a background check on me. I'm sure it'll come back with an all clear."

They all relaxed and smiled. "That's good to know," Markus offered and gestured to the menu she held. "Are you ready to order?"

"An egg white omelet and an espresso, please."

"Good choice."

When Markus strode off, Mitch and Eddie leaned in. "How did you know to order the egg white omelet? You've just made a friend."

"Really? Is there a story behind that?"

"Hannah is the chef here and she introduced the egg white omelet but it's not exactly everyone's favorite dish. Your order will make her happy and anything that makes her happy makes Markus happy. So, we're in for a good day."

Abby grinned. "I'm glad I could help out."

"A word of warning," Eddie said, "Don't order it at Joyce's. She'll grumble."

"Too late. I already tried, but she went easy on me and actually suggested I come here."

"She must like you. Joyce doesn't care for compromises," Eddie said. "So, why are you researching cyanide?"

Mitch nudged his sister. "That's what the killer used."

Abby shrugged. "I want to know how the killer procured it. Is it readily accessible to him because it's something he... or she, uses in their business, or is it something he had to hunt down?"

Mitch grinned. "We heard you accused Bartholomew Carr. That took some backbone. I didn't think you'd go through with it."

"I... I didn't do it on purpose," Abby said as Markus set a large plate in front of her.

"Enjoy."

"Thank you."

"So, if you didn't kill Dermot," Markus said, "Should we be on the alert for a poisoner?"

"It wouldn't hurt to take precautions. Having said that, I don't want to be responsible for inciting suspicion." Abby showed them the photo she'd taken of Dermot and some of his lady friends. "Do any of these people come to the pub?"

Eddie studied the photo. "Everyone in Eden comes to The Gloriana."

Markus leaned in for a closer look. "Everyone except her." He pointed at the woman in the background, the one Abby had labeled person of interest.

Eddie had another look. "I've seen her around." She clicked her fingers. "I know her name but I can't think of it now. It'll come to me." Eddie looked up. "So who else do you suspect?"

"What do you know about Annabelle Hugh?"

On the way back to her room, Abby tried to contact Joshua Ryan. When she got his answering service she left a message asking him what sort of tea had been found in the teapot.

"It's only me," Abby said as she eased the door open gently. Doyle's head popped up on the armrest. "Yep, it's safe to come out. Let's go out for a bit." She snuck him out of the pub and dropped him off at the Gazette.

"Look after him?" Faith asked. "Yes, please. But why don't you want him along?"

"I need to check on some people and they might not be amenable to the idea of Doyle walking into their store."

A short while later, Abby stood outside Annabelle Hugh's Jewelry store—her first port of call. The storefront was dedicated to fantasy items. Abby spent a few minutes pretending to admire the display while casting her glance around to get the lay of the land.

Eddie and Mitch had given her some basic information about Annabelle. She'd studied jewelry design and had inherited the store from her uncle. She'd spent some time overseas. She'd had dreams of making it big and traveling the world but had ended up settling here. According to Eddie, there had been a man involved and a severe case of heartbreak. If Abby stayed on, that would make two people who'd come here to lick their wounds.

Catching sight of a tall, elegant woman, Abby tried to determine her age. Late fifties? Early sixties? "Did you want Dermot dead, Annabelle?" Abby wondered in a soft whisper. The fact cyanide was used in jewelry making made her a suspect, but without a motive, it wouldn't stick.

She hadn't seen photos of her and Dermot together, but that didn't mean anything. The night before, Sebastian had told her about the people involved in the committee responsible for allocating funds. When he'd mentioned Annabelle's name, Abby had noticed a slight hesitation in his voice. When she'd asked him about it, Sebastian had shrugged. According to him, Annabelle hadn't always seen eye to eye with Dermot, often voting against him when he'd suggested supporting causes that were not artistic in nature.

Knowledge is power, but she had to be careful what she did with that power, Abby thought and strode inside. Annabelle specialized in silver and had several display cases full of her beautiful wares, from elegant designs to artistic showy pieces. Again, Abby made a point of admiring the displays. All part of her cover, she thought.

"Can I help you?" a cultured voice asked.

Abby turned and smiled. The woman oozed stylish elegance, from her tidy bob that teased her shoulders to the beige suit she wore.

When Annabelle's pleasant smile wavered, Abby assumed she'd just been struck by a joining of the dots moment.

"You're that reporter going around accusing people of killing Dermot. How could you be so heartless? Do you have any idea what Dermot meant to this community?"

"That's why I'm asking questions," Abby offered. "Don't you want to know who killed him?"

"Let the police do their job. You can only get in the way."

Annabelle Hugh did not look like the type of person who'd back down so Abby went on the attack. "What are you hiding? Is there something you don't want me to find out?"

To her surprise, Annabelle hesitated before speaking, "Dermot's death has come as a shock to the community. You wouldn't understand how much he meant to us all. He's gone, but we're still protective of him."

Yes, she kept hearing that, but someone had suspended their strong feelings long enough to commit murder. "Then you should be doing all you can to assist anyone looking into his death. I'm not after a story. Like you, I want the killer caught." As she spoke, Abby had to take a deep swallow. She hadn't met Dermot in person, at least not while he'd been alive, but there'd been an instant connection. When she'd spoken with him on the phone, it had felt as though they'd known each other for a long time and were just catching up.

If the killer turned out to be a local, they'd all be in for another shock. It would take them a long time to get over it, if ever. This could change everyone's perception of their neighbors in this little town.

Annabelle lifted her chin. "It can't possibly be one of us. It isn't."

"You often clashed with Dermot."

Annabelle's lips quivered. "You think that gave me reason to kill him?"

Abby's encounter with Richard Armstrong proved to be equally fruitless, but she did enjoy herself from the moment she saw him emerging from the back room of his studio, dressed as a country squire about to set out on a hunting trip.

Not a fashion statement, Abby thought as she noticed his tweed jacket had aged to keep up with his fifty odd years. His dark hair had a sprinkling of gray and a few lines crisscrossed his chiseled features. Abby couldn't help wondering why men always looked more distinguished with gray in their hair.

"They warned me you might come by." His smile told her he found it all too amusing, but his furrowed brow suggested he would play along.

"When was the last time you saw Dermot?"

"Alive or dead?" he asked.

Abby huffed out a breath. "Let me guess, you've been talking with Mitch Faydon."

He nodded. "Had a drink with him. I can't remember a time when we had so much to talk about. What with Dermot's death and your arrival. Did you happen to take a photo of the scene?"

"No. Why would I?" Abby kicked herself for sounding so defensive.

"You're a reporter. Isn't it in your nature?"

"Out of curiosity, is that what you would have done?"

He folded his arms and stared up at the ceiling. "Hard to say. My instinct might have kicked in but then,

I'm sure I would have been too shocked by the scene to react. What did you do?"

"I called emergency services, of course." And then she'd gone into shock. Just as well she'd never aspired to become a front-line reporter. "How often do you handle arsenic?"

He laughed. "You can't be serious. This is the digital age."

She looked around his store. "So, you keep these old cameras as keepsakes."

"The studio is as old as the town. The cameras came with the business when I purchased it a dozen years ago. I used to have a business in the city but then I decided to slow down and go into semi-retirement. I kept the cameras but not the equipment used to develop films."

"I don't suppose you noticed anyone acting suspiciously or overheard someone…" she shrugged. "Sorry. I'm grasping at straws." And now that everyone seemed to know her business, she was fast on her way to becoming a laughing stock. "Hang on. I saw a photograph at the pub of the Faydon siblings. It looked old."

He nodded. "As I said. Digital. I can make an old photograph look new and vice versa."

"Where's Doyle?" Joyce Breeland asked. "I told you he could come in."

"Hello to you too." Abby smiled at Joyce's invitation to join her at her corner table.

"You've only been here a couple of days and we already expect to see you two together. I hope you haven't given him away."

Would she give him away? Abby shrugged. "I bought him a coat and a harness. I think that means I'm getting attached, which is probably unfair to him. Even if I stay, it'll only be for a year."

"That's what everyone says at first," Joyce murmured as she dug inside her pocket. "I have the list you wanted. Also, we went through the list Faith put together for you and everyone checks out. They all came into the café the morning in question."

"Is this normal?" Or had people made a point of making an appearance in town to establish some sort of alibi?

Joyce chortled. "Normal? A lot of people stick to a weekly schedule, meaning I definitely see them on a specific day of the week, but they also come in on other days. I do, after all, make the best coffee in the district."

Abby still found it odd that they'd all come into the café that morning. Yes, almost as if they needed to be seen. She placed an order for coffee and a muffin and inspected the beverages menu. "You serve a variety of teas."

"Some customers are adventurous," Joyce said, "They stock a generic brand at home but they come in here to try something new."

"Including Dermot?"

Taking a sip of her tea, Joyce studied her over the rim of her cup. "He bought his tea from me. He preferred strong flavored ones. Last week he was trying out Assam Black. It's a classic Indian variety with a strong malty taste."

Perfect for disguising the almond taste of cyanide. Although, Abby rather liked the idea of Dermot having a gun pointed at him and being forced to drink the poison.

"The week before it was Kandy," Joyce continued. "The blend has quite a robust flavor. But then he moved onto Oolong. A more subtle blend. He was intrigued by the fact you could steep it several times and each infusion produced a distinctive taste." Joyce shrugged. "Dermot appreciated the little things in life."

"Did you recommend those teas?"

"Meaning, did I steer him toward a strong flavored tea?" Joyce paused as if for effect. Setting her cup down, she gave her a small smile. "He asked, and I provided."

Okay, so she needed to follow the trail of tea. "Do you get all your tea from the same supplier?"

Joyce nodded.

Looking over at the counter, Abby noted several large glass containers. "Did the tea come pre-packed or loose leaf?"

"I don't normally sell to the public but I made an

109

exception for Dermot. He'd come in and buy enough for the week. Am I a suspect now?"

Abby frowned. "Do you want to be?" she asked casting an admiring glance at Joyce's 1950's style red and white floral dress. Abby couldn't help thinking Joyce looked like a dark-haired version of June Cleaver.

"If I am, I'd like to be cleared." Joyce chuckled lightly. "I'm actually having fun. I've never been inter-rogated before."

"It's a fact-finding exercise. I'm not the police." They looked at each other for long minutes. "Has anyone else drank the Assam Black this week?" Abby finally asked.

"One other customer and, as far as I know, she's still alive. Maybe I should pull it off the shelf, just to be on the safe side, and have it tested."

When her cell phone rang, Abby checked the caller ID. "Sorry, it's Joshua Ryan." She answered and had to listen to the detective lecturing her on the dangers of accusing people of murder. "I did no such thing. Bartholomew Carr simply reacted to an innocent question. Now that I think about it, he actually overreacted. Isn't that a sign of guilt? You know, the lady... or in this case, the man, doth protest too much. You should arrest him. And, before you warn me not to tell you how to do your job, I want to know if you've tested the tea in the pot."

"Yes, that's how we confirmed Dermot ingested it," Joshua said.

Abby already knew that because Sebastian had told her. "I mean, what sort of tea was it? There are many varieties. Last night, I noticed he had quite a few different canisters of tea." Abby refrained from mentioning Joyce's name and role in supplying Dermot with tea.

"Why do you want to know?"

"A strong flavored tea would disguise the taste of cyanide. If the tea he drunk had a more subtle flavor, then we might have to consider the possibility someone forced him to drink it. Otherwise, he would have picked up on the taste and not drunk it."

"We?" Joshua Ryan asked. "Have you been tossing ideas around with someone else?"

Did he sound annoyed because she'd dared to play with someone else or because he thought she was putting herself in danger?

"I meant you, the police. The people investigating the murder. That reminds me. Was there a second cup of tea?" Abby listened to the silence. Then came an intake of breath.

"When exactly did I start sharing information with you?" he asked.

Abby grinned. "We're having a friendly conversation and sharing ideas. What if I give you a solid lead? Are you going to turn your back on that?"

"Withholding information can get you into serious trouble," he warned.

"So... Did you find a second cup?"

"No."

"Did June say if she'd prepared the tea before she left?"

"Yes, she did. Before you ask, the answer is no. She didn't have any tea. I'll look into the blend of tea and get back to you."

"You will?"

He chuckled.

"You're humoring me."

"Talk to you soon. And, in case I forgot to mention it, don't leave town."

Abby disconnected the call and tried to remember why Joshua Ryan had called.

"Please explain the frown," Joyce said.

Abby waved her hand. "I've been chastised for stirring the hornet's nest." She told Joyce about her encounter with the artist.

"He's a sensitive soul and wouldn't harm a fly," Joyce assured her.

Remembering the photos she'd taken the night before, Abby showed them to Joyce and asked if she could put names to faces.

"Oh, I remember that day. First day of spring. That's Norma Reed on his right and Liz Hamilton, the retired school teacher."

"And what about that woman in the background?"

Joyce hummed. "Oh, yes. That's Felicia Williams. She bought a farm a few years back as a weekend retreat. Then she decided to move here permanently. I don't really know much about her. She tends to keep to herself and... She's not really the chatty type."

"Looking at the photo I can't help thinking she disapproves of Dermot."

"You're right. She's not the friendliest soul around. In the time she's been here I don't think she's made any friends. I tried breaking the ice, but..." Joyce shrugged, "I'm not everyone's cup of tea, either. Some people think I'm a bit odd."

"You are unique." Abby studied the photo. "Is she staring at Dermot or at the women? I can't quite decide."

"She's definitely burning a hole in someone's head."

"Do you know if she had any contact with Dermot?" Abby asked.

"Dermot made a point of talking with everyone, but I can't say that I ever saw them together." Joyce finished her tea. "Are you going to tell Joshua about her?"

Abby smiled. "I'll play it by ear. After all, he more or less warned me to stay away." Hard to say if he'd been serious. Surely, he could see the benefit of her sharing her own point of view.

"He might think you're onto something."

Abby tilted her head. "I think you might be right." Now she had to figure out which tidbit of information he'd found interesting.

Chapter Eleven

*D*oyle rushed toward her, his eyes bright, his tail wagging.

"Someone's happy to see you," Faith said looking up from her desk. "You'd think you'd been separated for ages. Look at his tail. If it wags any faster he might take off."

Abby stooped down, and laughed as Doyle rolled onto his back, presumably putting in a request for a belly rub, which she happily provided. "Did he behave?"

"He fell asleep at my feet. I tried to play catch with him, but he wasn't interested."

Abby exchanged a knowing look with Doyle. "Next time, try talking to him. I think he likes it."

"Really? My dogs only pay attention to me when I bring out a ball."

Abby drew out her cell phone and showed Faith the

photo she'd taken at Dermot's house. "I forgot to show you this earlier. Do you recognize anyone?"

"Yes, all of them."

Abby pointed at the woman in the background. "Including Felicia Williams?"

Faith nodded. "Unlike you, she's still easing into life in Eden."

"Unlike me? What do you mean?"

"Well, you arrived and made an instant splash," Faith explained. "Everyone already knows you. Felicia started out spending her weekends here. Then she moved here permanently, or so we think. I doubt anyone can say they've had a conversation with her and she doesn't take part in any of the town activities." Faith took a closer look at the photo. "Wow. Look at the way she's glaring at Dermot."

"What makes you think she's looking at him?"

Faith grinned. "The trajectory of her gaze." She searched her drawer and produced a ruler. "See. Her eyes are aimed directly at him."

"Okay. Let's play with this. What do you know about Felicia? She's not sitting with the group, but did she ever socialize with Dermot?"

"Hard to say. Dermot talked to everyone."

"Everyone except Donovan Carmichael and his gossipy neighbor, Thelma Harrison," Abby said under her breath.

"It's not that he never talked to Thelma. He simply

steered clear of her. As for Felicia, I never heard him say she visited him at home."

"Are you sure about that?"

Faith nodded. "He'd always comment on what was going on in his life. You know, general remarks such as so and so dropped in for a cup of tea, she's looking great. As far as Dermot was concerned, everyone always looked great."

"Would June Laurie know anything more about what went on at Dermot's place?" The cleaning lady might have acted as a sounding board for Dermot. Then again, as Faith had said, Dermot hadn't cared for gossiping.

"I guess you'll have to ask her. In fact, I'm surprised you haven't already approached her."

"Joshua spoke with her a couple of times, I didn't want to risk harassing her."

Faith grinned and bobbed her eyebrows up and down. "It's Joshua now, is it?"

"Don't read too much into it. Since arriving in Eden, I've met so many people, I need to try to remember all their names but saying Detective Inspector Joshua Ryan is a bit of a mouthful."

"I guess it's too soon to ask if there's someone special in your life, someone you left behind?"

Abby gave her a brisk smile. "Yeah, too soon. What if I leave tomorrow or next week? The less you know about me, the sooner I'll fade away from your memory." She searched her handbag for a pen and piece of paper and, annoyingly, came up empty. "Do you have a spare notebook and pen, please? I filled up my little notebook when I interviewed Bartholomew."

"Are you going to draw up a crime storyboard?"

"A what?"

Faith shrugged. "I've seen it on TV. The detectives always draw up a timeline of events. They step back from it and start telling a story. Hence the storyboard." Faith clicked her fingers. "There's a whiteboard in the storage room. I'll go get it. The Gazette could be our brainstorming headquarters."

Abby looked at Doyle and said, "Someone's been watching too much TV."

Moments later, Faith reappeared wheeling a whiteboard in. "I have markers in my top drawer." Grabbing the ruler, she set about drawing a straight line across the whiteboard. "June left at nine in the morning and you arrived at Dermot's just before midday."

"Joshua pinpointed 11.30 as the estimated time of death," Abby said. "Approximately half an hour before I arrived." June had left at nine that morning, the killer stepped in, poisoned Dermot and two and a half hours later, he died.

Faith shook her head. "I can't believe our local gossip, Thelma, didn't see anyone else entering the house. She spends her life sitting by the window."

"Perhaps she was distracted by something," Abby offered. "At some point, she would have to take a toilet break or get up to make herself a cup of tea or coffee."

"True. We'll have to get her to admit to it. It won't be easy. She takes great pride in being a busybody."

"She must live in a small world. What could she possibly expect to see from that vantage point? Poe Lane is not exactly Grand Central Station."

Faith wrote down the times they had pinpointed. "She does mix it up a bit. At lunch, she goes to the main street and either buys something to take home or she sits at Joyce's. I've often seen her sitting by the window. Rarely, if ever, outside because of her pale skin."

Abby tugged her hair back. "Let me guess. Most people get out and about after lunch?"

"Yes." Faith tapped the whiteboard. "What else do we have?"

"We also have a list drawn up by Joyce and her staff placing several people at her café." Abby waved the piece of paper Joyce had given her.

Faith stepped back and studied the list of names they had on the board. "I'm going to try to remember if I saw anyone walking past the newspaper. There's always someone waving at me. It's just a matter of sifting through all the debris floating around in my mind. I might have seen someone striding by in a hurry and not made the connection." Faith jumped back.

"What?"

"Oh, I was just trying to walk a mile in the killer's shoes. Picture this, the killer has just witnessed Dermot drawing his last breath, he realizes what he's done and, panicking, he runs." Faith pressed her hands to her cheeks. "If the killer is a woman, she might have shrieked and rushed out of the house. Along the way, she would have told herself to act normal and pretend as if nothing had happened. Distracted by her thoughts and the shock of her actions, she might have stumbled or collided with someone." Faith then proceeded to act out the scene.

"Wow, you're good."

Faith grinned. "I belong to the local theater group, the Eden Thespians. We put on annual productions. Hey, we should do Mousetrap." Faith scribbled a reminder on the edge of the board. "I'll have to suggest it at our next production meeting."

Abby tried to picture someone fleeing the scene of the crime but something told her Dermot's death had not been a careless crime of passion. The killer had put some thought into it—a lot of thought, since he hadn't been spotted by the local gossip. Could he have made his getaway through a back door or window?

Faith shook her head. "Ugh! I can see a parade of people strolling by inside my head."

"Try to remember something about the day," Abby suggested. "Something you always do in the morning and take it from there. Are there any regulars you see strolling by every day?"

"Sure. Plenty of them. Jolly Maeve is one. She can have her city paper delivered right to her front doorstep but she chooses to walk to the store to get it. Otherwise, she'd never get any exercise. I see her every day at about ten in the morning."

"Did you see her this morning?" Abby asked.

Faith was about to answer but stopped. "I want to say I did, but I also want to be sure. The mind can play tricks." Faith grumbled under her breath. "Oh, heavens. I'd need to undergo some sort of regression hypnosis. I honestly can't tell you with absolute certainty if I saw Jolly or not. And now this doubt is probably convincing my mind I didn't see her." Faith swung toward her desk. "I'm going to call her and find out."

Abby studied the board. Taking a marker pen, she worked on a bullet point list.

"Yes," Faith said. "Jolly strode by and waved but said I barely glanced up and, like you, she also saw me talking with Donovan Carmichael the other day." Faith looked at the board. "What's that?"

"It's what I remember. When I arrived at Dermot's house, there was a piano tune playing. I've heard it before but I can't place it and please don't ask me to hum it. I don't even sing in the shower for fear I might shatter the windows."

"Was it a jazz tune? Classical? Modern?"

"Not modern and not classical. Sort of not classical. I'd recognize it if I heard it again."

Faith held up a finger. "I have a list of music Dermot had selected for his funeral service."

"I doubt a name will help."

Faith grinned. "Oh, but I have something better. It's

not just a list. It's a compilation. I have it on my phone. Here it is."

Faith clicked through the playlist, checking with Abby to see if anything sounded familiar.

"That one."

Faith nodded. "It's a French composer. Erik Satie. Dermot loved listening to him on Sundays."

"But I went to his house on Monday."

"Then it couldn't have been this one because when I say Dermot only listened to it on Sundays, I meant it. Dermot loved routine. He said it turned his tasks into something mundane so he didn't have to think about them." Abby must have looked confused because Faith went on to explain, "In his opinion, why waste time deciding what you're going to listen to? His entire wardrobe had been laid out in such a way he only needed to work from left to right. If the weather didn't agree with the selection of clothes, he merely eliminated or added. Monday's suit had the option to add a woolen vest or sweater and so on."

Abby thought about her process for choosing what she'd wear and cringed. "I usually dive in and grab whatever is there."

"Yeah, me too," Faith admitted. "Okay, I do give it a little thought, but I'm not anything like Joyce Breeland."

"I noticed she takes great care with her clothes. What's up with that? Since arriving, I haven't seen her dressed in anything that belongs to this century."

"You should see her on movie nights. Sometimes we all dress up. Film noire nights are fun. For the last one, I went dressed as a gangster's moll."

"Yes, but... Joyce doesn't seem to restrict her dress-up days to movie nights."

"That's what we love about her. She adds a vibrant splash of color to life in Eden and we love her for it."

Abby tugged the sleeve of her jacket. "I suddenly feel self-conscious." For as long as she could remember, she'd opted to wear jeans matched with a blouse or T-shirt and a tailored jacket.

"You look great and I'm not just saying that to make you feel good," Faith remarked.

Doyle's attention skipped from Faith to Abby and then he yawned.

"We either confused Doyle or we bored him." Abby turned back to the whiteboard and tried to remember what they'd been talking about before the subject of clothes had interfered.

"Music and Dermot's habit of sticking to a routine," Faith said almost as if she'd read her mind. "What can I say? I'm a great personal assistant."

"Do you know if that tune held any sentimental value? Maybe we could connect it to someone from his past. There has to be a reason why he broke with routine."

"Where's your mind going with this?" Faith asked.

"Well, imagine the killer, someone acquainted with Dermot, pays him a visit. He's a regular visitor, or maybe someone he hasn't caught up with in a long while. They reminisce and the visitor asks if he still listens to that same tune every Sunday. When Dermot tells him that yes, he does, the visitor suggests listening to it."

"Why?"

"Because the tune has some sort of significance."

Faith cupped her chin. "Such as?"

"It could have been the tune playing when Dermot saw his wife for the first time. This other person had been keen on her, but he'd been dragging his feet. Dermot, however, acted quickly and snatched her for himself."

"Giving the killer a motive. Jealousy and revenge," Faith said. "You're assuming the killer is a man."

"Point taken. It could be a woman, in which case, she might have talked about the first time they'd met and she would have secretly regretted or resented having missed her opportunity with Dermot. Her motive would be resentment. Despite being a widower and available, he's still not interested in her."

"Have you done this before?" Faith asked.

Abby shook her head. "No, but I've read a lot of mysteries. Revenge and jealousy appear to be great motivators for murder."

Faith grinned. "That's the first bit of personal infor-mation you've revealed. Does that mean you're staying on?"

"It simply means I wanted you to understand I don't

have a natural devious bone in my body. I can't think like a killer because I've never personally entertained thoughts of killing anyone." Abby flinched.

"Are you sure about that? Is there something you want to share with me because confession is good for the soul?"

"No." She'd killed a suit, but that didn't count. "If I send you this photo, can you print it out?"

"Quick change of subject and, yes. I'm sure Sebastian won't accuse me of misappropriating company supplies or time."

"Did Dermot mind?"

Faith chortled. "No. He wasn't petty. Sorry, I... I had a phone interview this morning for an office position."

"I guess it didn't go too well for you."

"They wanted to know how I felt about taking a company pen home and having coffee breaks outside of scheduled times."

"What did you say?"

A splotch of red spread across Faith's cheeks. "I hate being put on the spot. I didn't want to lie."

Abby laughed.

"It's not funny. Where am I going to find a job like this one? I told them I had another call coming through and would get back to them."

"At least you're honest about not wanting to lie."

"Yes, but that won't pay my bills."

Abby typed in the email address, attached the photo and hit send.

Faith swung into action and produced a photocopy of the photo. "Shall I do the honors and pin it up on the board?"

"Yes, please. Now to find out where Felicia Williams lives." At some point, she wanted to pay her a visit.

"And why would you want to know that?"

Both Abby and Faith swung around.

Abby smiled. "Aha! Just the man I wanted to see."

Chapter Twelve

"This is breaking and entering. I'm an officer of the law. I can't be seen doing this."

"Relax. Doyle is keeping watch. Besides, I have the front door key and permission from the owner. Hold steady while I try to climb the fence. I don't want my jeans to rip."

"I'm taking a photo of this," Faith said. "The local detective helping a possible murder suspect to break into Dermot's house. No one will believe me."

"Hey, I'm not a suspect," Abby complained.

Faith shrugged. "The caption has to be interesting enough to grab people's interest."

"Remind me again why I've been fooled into helping you break the law?" Joshua asked.

"Because I'm a foot taller than Faith and she wouldn't be able to give me a hand up. Now, put your back into it. Heave-ho." Abby made a grab for the top of the fence.

Joshua grunted. "This is ridiculous. Come down. I'm going to try myself."

"Hey guys..."

"I know I can do this," Abby insisted. "And why is this fence so high? Don't people in this town trust each other?"

Faith tried to get their attention again. "Guys."

"Hang on, Faith. I'm nearly there." Gritting her teeth, Abby pulled herself up another inch. "If the local gossip swears she didn't see anyone going in through the front door, other than me, then the killer must have jumped the fence. It stands to reason, and if the killer can do it, so can I."

"I'll tell you what else stands to reason," Faith murmured. "We're standing in the alley, therefore, there must be a back gate leading to the alley, and guess what? Here it is."

"Huh?" As Abby turned, she wobbled, lost her balance and toppled over Joshua.

"Thank you. This photo is sure to amuse everyone."

Abby dusted herself off. "Hey! You can't have fun at my expense. Think of my reputation. What will people say about me?"

"You'll live."

Joshua cleared his throat. "Can we go in now? I'd feel better if we didn't stand around out here waiting to be caught red-handed."

"You'd make a dreadful criminal," Abby murmured.

They made their way into the backyard. A cast iron garden table and chairs setting sat on a paved area under the shade of a tall Eucalyptus tree with lush green ferns surrounding it all. The perfect setting for an afternoon tea. Noticing Joshua wasn't even bothering to inspect the backyard, Abby frowned. "Hey." She saw him struggling to keep a straight face. "Hey. Wait a minute. You knew about the back gate."

Faith laughed. "Thank you for providing me with the best story for our movie night. Joyce usually has the best ones, but I believe this will trump anything she can come up with. You'll be talked about for years to come."

"I thought we were helping each other," Abby growled as she strode past him.

He laughed. "I don't know where you got that idea from."

"So why are you here?" Abby asked.

"To stop you from getting into trouble." He sighed. "All right. For the amusement factor. I couldn't help it. It's been a long day and I needed to decompress."

"A long day or a slow day in Eden?" Mitch Faydon had given her a taste of what happened when life in Eden ground to a snail's pace. She'd have to watch out or she'd become an easy target.

Turning back, she looked at the paved path leading from the rear gate. "I guess there's no point in asking if the killer left any footprints."

"None. We searched the alley and didn't find anything."

"Do we assume the killer came in the back way because he wanted to avoid detection, or can we be flexible and entertain other ideas? Maybe the killer had a habit of coming in through the back. They were old friends and he didn't need permission and he used the gate because it was a shortcut for him."

"Or her," Faith murmured.

"Yes, it could be a woman. In fact, isn't poison the weapon of choice for female killers?"

Joshua nodded. "Although, every killer likes to create their own statistics."

"You're talking about career criminals and serial killers. Does that mean you're linking Dermot's death to the other ones that have been reported?"

"We don't have any reason to."

That could only mean the other deaths hadn't been the result of cyanide or a similar poison.

"Where are you going?" Joshua asked when Abby let herself in through the back door.

"I need to get some of Dermot's journals. I have Sebastian's permission." She noticed Joshua frowning. Abby laughed. "What? Are you worried you missed something?"

"We have his laptop."

"Aha, but Dermot had his quirks. According to Sebastian, he also enjoyed making handwritten notes." Belatedly, Abby realized she might not really want to share such pertinent information. "I assume your off-duty status prevents you from confiscating any important information I might stumble upon?"

"You can assume, but you'd be dead wrong. A police officer is never off duty."

They made their way toward the study, with Doyle sniffing his way in front of them. "I think Doyle is trying to prove himself useful. Hey, Doyle. Are you trying to impress the detective in the hope he'll adopt you as the police mascot?"

Doyle lifted his nose in the air and trotted off.

"You hurt his feelings," Faith said. "Why would you ask him that? He's probably putting two and two together and thinking you want to get rid of him."

Abby looked at Joshua who gave her a shrug.

"I'm with Faith. Dogs are sensitive and intuitive. I guess you've never had one."

No pets allowed in the house. The words echoed in her mind. "My mom was allergic to them."

They all stood in front of a floor to ceiling bookcase. The antique desk in front of it suggested Dermot enjoyed easy access to the neat stack of notebooks. Abby picked one up and admired the leather binding. "This looks handcrafted."

"There are over fifty of them. Where do we start?" Faith asked.

"You take one end, I'll take the other and Joshua can tackle the ones in the middle."

"What? Right here? Now?" he asked.

"Unless you have a better suggestion. That reminds me. Why didn't the police take these in as possible evidence?"

"I had someone go through them and he didn't find anything."

"Let's hope, for his sake, we don't find something." Abby skimmed through the first few pages. "This reads like an index to his day. It states the weather and all the people he encountered throughout the day. Alongside the names, he also included brief notes. Agnes Richards. In hospital for hip replacement operation. Send flowers."

"I remember that day," Faith said, "Dermot came in to the office late saying he'd had to swing by the florist to organize flowers."

Abby flipped ahead to the latest entries until she found a note about the first phone conversation she'd had with him. Delightful and charming, should be a great addition to our little town, it read.

"Why are you frowning?" Faith asked.

Abby remembered the conversation she'd had with Dermot. From the start, he'd left her in no doubt the job was hers for the taking. She'd been torn about moving so far away for a new job and leaving all her friends and family behind but talking with Dermot had set her at ease making it a little easier to deal with the residual misgivings for being forced to make the decision. She'd enjoyed her job and lifestyle in Seattle and had never imagined needing to move away.

"We've got our work cut out for us. The killer's name is in one of these notebooks." She slanted her gaze toward Joshua in time to see the slight lift of his lips. "Tell me again why you dropped in at the Gazette?"

He smiled. "My sixth sense told me to."

Grabbing a couple of notebooks, Abby sank down on a nearby chair. Faith leaned against a bookcase, while Joshua made himself comfortable at Dermot's desk.

An hour later, Sebastian found them all still going through the notebooks. He stood by the door, his hands hitched on his hips. "Did I forget about inviting you all here?"

Abby checked her watch. "Heavens. Look at the time." She set the notebook down and stretched. "I suggest we call it a night and resume our search tomorrow."

Joshua laughed under his breath. "I'm afraid I'll have to bow out. I actually have a job to get to."

Doyle stirred awake, looked around, and curled up again only to do a double take. Seeing Sebastian standing by the door, he gave a half-hearted woof.

"That's an efficient guard dog you have there," Sebastian said.

"Hush. He's still recovering from a bad experience." Abby bent down to pick him up and strode out saying, "I'm headed to the pub. I could do with some food.

Does anyone want to join me?" When she turned, she saw them all following her, including Sebastian.

"I don't want to miss out on anything," Faith said, "So I'll call my neighbor and ask her to check in on my dogs. They won't be happy about me coming home late, but they have to understand mom has to eat too. And all that is probably more information than you all need."

Abby stopped at the front door. "Hang on. I should take some of those journals to look over tonight. Knowing me, I'll wake up in the middle of the night with a sparkly idea."

Sebastian hunted down a bag and filled it up for her.

When they reached the pub, Abby said, "You two cover me. I need to sneak Doyle inside. They don't know I have a dog."

Joshua chortled. "And you don't want to tell them because you're afraid they'll evict you?"

They all laughed, including Sebastian who suggested, "Why don't you try something daring. Walk right in and pretend Doyle isn't a dog."

"And if they kick you out, you could come stay with me," Faith suggested. "I have a spare bedroom and my dogs will love a new playmate. My cat, Cleopatra, will be snooty at first, but she won't scratch him."

Hypothetically, by the end of the night, she could be both jobless and homeless. Clearly, she hadn't given this much thought. Abby looked over at the residents' entrance. She'd stand a better chance going in that way since it bypassed the pub and led straight to the apartments upstairs.

"Where's the fun in that?" Joshua said and gave her a nudge toward the main entrance.

With Faith leading the way, and Sebastian and Joshua bringing up the rear, they swept her into the pub. The buzz of conversation mellowed only slightly. Behind the bar, Mitch gave her a small nod. Abby had tugged her jacket around Doyle. She didn't think Mitch had seen him and if Markus, who sat by the fireplace, his legs stretched out, his fingers steepled under his chin, noticed the bundle in her arms, he didn't let on.

"So far, so good." Doyle appeared to make himself smaller in her arms, burying his little head in the crook of her arm.

"You're doing great," Sebastian said behind her. "Let's head over to the corner table."

They settled down and when a waitress approached them, they all ordered beers.

A moment later, Joshua murmured, "Heads up. Mitch is bringing the drinks over. Look alive, people."

Setting the drinks down, Mitch nodded and, instead of moving on, he wrapped his hand around the back of Abby's chair. "Are you all here to celebrate catching the killer?"

"Not quite," Abby said, her tone slightly strained, "We're getting closer."

Mitch turned to Sebastian and gave him a small nod. "I'm glad you came in. Saves me the trouble of hunting you down. We're holding a wake for Dermot here tomorrow night."

"I'll be here," Sebastian said.

"Are you all ready to order?" Mitch asked. He swept his gaze around the table. When he got to Abby, he held her gaze, his eyes twinkling with that spark of mischief she'd seen the first day she'd arrived. "How are you settling in, Abby Maguire? Are you making yourself right at home?" Mitch asked.

Abby tried to keep her gaze steady. If she looked away, she suspected she might end up looking down at Doyle who sat curled up on her lap. "Yes, I'm getting used to the place. Finding my way around... Meeting all the locals."

Mitch nodded. "If there's anything we can do to make your stay with us more homey, just let us know."

Joshua cleared his throat. "I'm ready to order."

"Yes, me too," Faith threw in.

They both looked at Sebastian who quickly picked up the menu. "Yes. I'm good to go."

Abby snatched the menu and bent her head to study it. "What to have. So many choices. Everything looks so good."

"You should try our T-bone steak," Mitch suggested. "Most customers ask for a doggy bag so they can take the bone home with them for their pets. The spare ribs are another favorite for pet owners. We prepare them two ways. American-style ribs and Argentinean-style short ribs served with a *salsa verde*. Or you could do the barbecue platter." Mitch hitched his thumb over to the next table, which was being served with one.

Abby marveled at the size of the platter and, taking a whiff, Doyle whimpered.

"That looks like a good choice," Joshua said.

They all agreed.

"Faith, I suppose you'll want a doggy bag."

"Oh, yes please. My doggies will love the bones."

Mitch looked at Abby who shrunk into her chair. "Okay, I'll put the order in for a barbecue platter."

Abby waited for Mitch to leave to say, "He knows."

"Oh, yes. He knows," they all agreed.

"I guess I should come clean."

Joshua shook his head. "It's too late now. Besides, that would really spoil the fun."

"Sorry, Doyle. I'm going to set you down on the floor, but you must promise to be quiet and stay out of sight." When Abby straightened, she found everyone looking at her.

Faith grinned. "You might want to start with 'stay' and 'sit'."

Abby lifted her chin. "Doyle is quite smart and understands more complex sentences. Excuse me, I need to use the restroom."

Along the way, she wondered what she'd do if Mitch asked her to get rid of Doyle. She couldn't imagine him doing it, but she'd only known him a few short days. If he'd noticed Doyle and if he had an issue with him...

Her mind raced ahead. How would Doyle fare on a long plane trip back home? As she stood washing her hands, someone came into the restroom. At first, Abby didn't make the connection but when the woman came out to wash her hands, Abby recognized her.

Felicia Williams, the woman with the killer gaze.

Chapter Thirteen

"**W**hat happened to you?" Faith half rose out of her chair. "You look pale. Did you have a close encounter with the pub's ghost?"

Abby looked over her shoulder. "There's a ghost here?"

"Rumor has it. Yes."

Abby shivered. "I... I bumped into Felicia Williams." Abby shivered again. "She wanted to know how I'd found Dermot." Catching her by surprise, the woman had fired one question right after the other, drilling her for information with the tenacity of the most seasoned reporter.

Looking over her shoulder, Abby saw Markus still sitting by the fireplace. She remembered showing him the photo she'd taken at Dermot's house. Markus had looked at it and had said everyone in the picture came to the pub, everyone except Felicia. He hadn't identified her by name because... no one really knew her. So why had she come tonight?

Faith laughed. "Did she think you had something to do with Dermot's death?"

"It's not funny. She seemed to think I killed him. She has beady eyes and at close range, they throw quite a punch." Abby didn't think she'd ever met anyone so embittered and she'd formed that impression even before Felicia had opened her mouth to speak. When she had, there'd been nothing but unkind, critical words for the people of Eden, including a harsh rebuke for Abby for presumably thinking she would fit in so quickly. Abby decided to withhold that information from the group. It had been bad enough hearing all the negatives; she certainly didn't want to be responsible for spreading them.

"Did you manage to get any questions in?" Faith asked. "She might be trying to throw you off the scent by projecting guilt."

"At the risk of sounding incompetent..." Right in front of a possible future employer... "No."

Sebastian gave her a lifted eyebrow look. "Nothing?"

"I'm... still suffering from jet lag." And not used to being intimidated. Although, there had been that one instance when a woman she'd interviewed for a home-style magazine article had insisted her cushions were covered in pure silk. Abby had already sneaked a look at the tag, which had revealed they'd been pure 100%

poly-something or other. The woman's fixed stare and hard tone had dared Abby to contradict her. She'd driven the message home by clicking her fingers, the prompt bringing her Rottweiler dogs to sit beside her.

Abby slumped back in her chair. Faith could be on to something. What if Felicia had been trying to cover up her own guilt by casting suspicion on her?

Seeing her close up, Felicia had actually looked familiar. Abby thought she must have seen her around town. If she had, it would come back to her.

Faith cleared her throat. "Um, Abby. We've waited for you but now you're here and the food is here... Can we start?"

"Oh, sure. You should have gone ahead and started without me." She scooped some potato salad into her plate and helped herself to some barbecue ribs. After several mouthfuls, she remembered Doyle.

Abby looked down. When she didn't see Doyle, she looked under the table. "Doyle?" she whispered hoping his doggy hearing would pick up her voice above the hum of conversation in the pub. Straightening, she said, "I don't see Doyle."

"He was curled up at my feet a moment ago," Faith said.

They all looked around.

Striding by their table, Mitch stopped. "Is something wrong?"

"I... I misplaced something." Sighing, Abby shook her head and stood up. "I'm sorry. Time to own up. I brought a dog in. He's only small and he's been through a bad time." She couldn't help wringing her hands. "Doyle. That's his name, although at first I called him Buddy. Katherine, who works at the vet's, told me he'd been registered at another clinic and his owner died. So poor Doyle has been all alone for over a month."

Mitch hitched his hands on his hips. "You brought a dog into the pub?"

She nodded. "I'm sorry. I don't know what I was thinking. I know there are regulations."

Mitch cleared his throat and went to stand by the bar. "Can I have everyone's attention, please?"

Conversation in the pub came to a halt and everyone turned toward Mitch.

"Has anyone seen a dog?" Mitch turned to Abby. "What type of dog is it?"

Abby cringed. "Pure bred mutt."

Raising his voice, Mitch said, "It's a pure-bred mutt and answers to Doyle."

Right on cue, everyone started calling out Doyle's name. A few people whistled. Behind her, Abby heard a gruff voice calling out Doyle's name. She turned and saw Markus standing there with Doyle in his arms. Doyle gave her a doggy grin.

"Doyle," Markus called out again.

Mitch called everyone's attention again. "Does anyone see a dog in the pub?"

Everyone looked at Markus holding Doyle in his arms. In unison, they all shook their heads and said no.

Mitch strode up to Markus. Taking Doyle, he handed him over to Abby. "If we see Doyle, we'll make sure to tell you about it."

"Thank you." Abby scurried over to the table and sat down. "I have no idea what just happened. Would anyone like to explain it to me?"

Joshua and Faith exchanged a look that appeared to share the same sentiment. "You've just been given a proper welcome."

"What does that mean?"

"It means, from here on in, you'll have to toe the line and be as strange as everyone else in Eden."

Could she be peculiar? Odd? Unusual?

Faith patted her hand. "Don't worry. I'll take you under my wing."

Abby leaned in. "Yes, but... Does this mean Doyle can stay with me?"

"Doyle?" they all asked, including Sebastian.

"My dog." Abby raised her eyebrows. Had she just claimed Doyle as her own?

"Dog? What dog? You know dogs are not allowed in the pub," Joshua said and gestured to a man sitting at the bar. "Robert Hopetown is a regular at the pub. He's the local health inspector. If he knew someone had brought a dog inside the pub, he would have issued a warning."

Abby looked over her shoulder and saw the health inspector raise his glass of beer at her in a salute.

Faith patted her hand again. "You'll catch on."

"Dig in before it gets cold," Joshua said as he helped himself to a slab of meat that would have had Fred Flintstone drooling.

Sebastian took a swig of his beer. "The French sure do know how to treat their dogs. No matter the breed, dogs can accompany their humans to restaurants and shops. If they can fit into a basket, they can go on public transport. Ironically, they are banned from public parks. It seems the idea of picking up after their pets hasn't quite caught on."

"Interesting," Abby said, "If I ever decide to get a dog, I'll have to think about moving to Paris."

"That's the spirit," Faith said between bites.

Markus approached their table and set a bowl of water down by Abby's chair. "In case that dog of yours ever turns up."

"Thank you."

As they all piled more food on their plates, Abby couldn't help thinking about Felicia. She had no idea what she hoped to find in Dermot's journals. The police had already gone through them and they were trained to sniff out anything suspicious.

It wouldn't hurt to have a fresh set of eyes looking through them, Abby thought. She'd keep her eyes peeled open for any mention of Felicia Williams. She had to be guilty of something. Also, Dermot might have made a note of something someone said. Poisoning someone didn't happen on the spur of the moment. If someone had been working on their nefarious plot, they might have let something slip.

Every few minutes, she looked down to make sure Doyle was still curled up by her feet. It seemed they'd been given a reprieve but she didn't want to push her luck. She didn't know much about dogs, but she figured Doyle could do with some stability and being with her right now seemed to be doing the trick.

With the meal over, they ordered coffee and a platter of profiteroles to share.

"If I eat one of those, I'll lay awake all night waiting for my heart attack," Abby said as she admired the small mountain of little cream puffs with delectable chocolate sauce swirled around them.

Faith helped herself to a couple. "You'll really like these. Hannah, that's the pub's chef, puts a splash of cognac in the cream. They're only bite size. It can't kill you."

Abby tried one. After the third one, Abby had to force herself to say no more. "Please tell me this is the one and only sweet she can bake."

"Hannah is spectacular in the kitchen and she's giving Joyce a run for her money, but don't tell Joyce I said that."

"I might have to take up jogging."

"You could try abstaining," Faith suggested.

"Oh, yeah? First you encourage me to indulge and now that I've acquired a taste, you tell me to abstain?"

"Or you could practice moderation. There's always a choice."

Abby grinned and helped herself to another profiterole. "I guess this is where Joyce and I stand together. I'm either all in, or... not." Indulging in the heavenly treat, she watched Joshua reading a message on his cell phone. "Are you going to share?"

Joshua gave her a brisk smile. "My dry-cleaning is ready to be collected."

"Really? I could have sworn you had your official police business deadpan look."

"Deadpan?" He smiled again.

"Now you're just trying to cover it up," Abby said.

Sebastian nodded. "Yes, I'd have to agree, you do the inscrutable look quite well."

Since he wasn't giving Sebastian an update, Abby decided to give him the benefit of the doubt. Although, she suspected he'd never give her a heads-up about a lead.

Faith turned to Sebastian. "Any idea what you'll do with Dermot's house? Sorry. That probably came across as insensitive."

"Don't worry about it. I haven't really given it any thought. Every square inch of the place is taken up with something that reminds me of him."

"Maybe you could pack it all up and store it at Castle Lodge," Faith suggested.

"I'm not sure Dermot would have approved," Sebastian said. "Castle Lodge is already packed to the rafters with family relics no one has any use for. Everything he had in his house he needed and used."

"Do you have someone looking after the other house?" Abby asked, even as she recalled Joyce mentioning a caretaker.

"We have a caretaker and a housekeeper." Sebastian chortled. "Sorry, nearly forgot. There is a Cavendish in residence. Cornelia."

They all waited for him to say more. When he didn't, Abby caved in to curiosity, but before she could say anything, Faith kicked her under the table and shook her head. Since Faith had already told her no one lived at the Lodge, Abby had to assume she had meant to say, certainly not anyone who could be mentioned because...

Cornelia was locked up in the attic?

Cornelia was the family skeleton everyone forgot to mention? Cornelia suffered from Miss Havisham syndrome?

There had to be a story there. Thinking about it, Abby lost the thread of the conversation. Then, out of the corner of her eye she caught sight of Felicia Williams leaving the pub. She wasn't alone. Another woman left with her. Abby reached for her cell phone but by the time she pointed it at the door to take a photo, they'd disappeared.

Joshua turned to look over his shoulder. "What was that about?"

Abby held up a finger calling for a moment while she tried to commit the woman's face to memory. She guessed she was the same age as Felicia, give or take a couple of years. Had Felicia wanted to be close to the hub of activity, hoping to catch any new developments in Dermot's case? She wished her reflexes hadn't failed her. If she'd taken a photo, she could have asked Faith if she recognized the other woman. "Felicia Williams just left with another woman and I don't mean to imply anything by that. From what I understand, it's unusual for her to come to the pub."

Joshua cleared his throat and looked away.

"You're keeping something from us."

"What would you say if I told you Felicia used to work as a chemist?"

A red flag sprung up in her mind. "I'd say, find out how long she'd known Dermot." Abby showed him the photo she'd taken at Dermot's house. "There's something going on there."

Sebastian leaned in for a closer look. "Yes, there's definitely some animosity."

Mitch approached them and set a couple of bags down on the table. "Doggy bags. One for you, Faith. And one for you, Abby." Mitch shrugged. "In case your dog ever turns up."

Abby didn't think she could keep up the pretense.

"Just thank the man," Faith whispered.

"Thank you. I'm sure Doyle will appreciate it... When... if he turns up."

"I hope he does soon," Mitch said. "We wouldn't want the local dog catcher to get him."

Faith smiled. "Before you know it, it'll become second nature to you."

Sebastian was the first to get up. "I need to walk off some of this dinner. I'll catch up with you tomorrow."

Joshua followed, "And I need to get an early start. If you find something useful, I'm sure your civic duty will take precedence." Joshua bent down and gave Doyle a scratch behind the ear. "Oh, and I hope your dog turns up."

Chapter Fourteen

*A*bby had stayed up half the night poring through Dermot's journals.

The next morning, she woke up to what sounded like rustling leaves and whimpering. Peeling an eye open, she saw pages scattered around her on the bed. She picked one up and squinted but couldn't make out the writing.

"I guess I took notes." She rolled over and felt something wet against her cheek. "Good morning. You should have woken me up, Doyle. You must be famished. Hey, how did you clamber up onto the bed? You're not big enough." The slight lift of his chin told her a different story. "We're buying you a bed today. I don't have anything against you sharing my bed, but I tend to toss and turn. I could squash you." He looked up at the ceiling and then gave her a distracted look. "Yeah? Whatever? If I didn't know better, I'd say you have an attitude. How old are you? Please tell me you're not a teenager. How will I ever keep up with you?"

She fed Doyle and then hurried through a shower. Since she'd missed breakfast at the pub, she grabbed a couple of journals and Doyle's leash and they headed out to Joyce's.

When they reached the café, Doyle pulled on the leash. "What? It's okay. Joyce said so."

Doyle didn't look convinced. He lowered his head and trotted a step behind Abby. When she sat down, he curled up at her feet under her chair.

"You're overreacting," she said as she scrolled through her messages. Two new ones had come in during the night. Her mom wanted her new address so she could send her a care package and some warm clothes. If Abby told her not to bother because she had everything she needed and wanted, her mom would suspect her of covering up her dire circumstances, so she replied with a brief message explaining she would forward an address as soon as she found somewhere to settle down. The other email made her frown. She considered deleting it straightaway but curiosity got the better of her.

What did her ex-boss want? After reading the first few lines, she set the cell phone down and sat there, staring into space.

Joyce's cheerful greeting shook her out of her reverie and took her mind off the email she'd just half read… "Hi."

"How are you doing?"

The concern in Joyce's tone caught Abby by surprise. "I'm... I'm fine."

"Are you sure? I heard about Doyle going missing. You must be beside yourself with worry. Poor little scamp, you only just found him. In your place, I'd be so worried I wouldn't be able to eat a bite."

Abby heard Doyle whimper. She knew she had a choice. She could either play along or put a stop to all this nonsense. Something told her the latter would cast her as an outsider. Did she want to be ostracized so soon after arriving?

"I'll need my energy to go looking for him."

Joyce nodded. "What would you like?"

"Blueberry Pancakes, please. They sound amazing." She cast her eye over the beverage menu. "I'll also have a Rise and Shine Espresso. Thank you."

"That's a quadruple espresso. Are you sure you're up to it?"

"I need it this morning."

Joyce handed the order to another waitress and then drew out a chair. "Any news about Dermot's killer?"

"Nothing. If Joshua is closing in on someone, he's not telling."

"Perhaps I can help." Joyce smiled. "I could threaten to ban him. No more coffee for him until he plays nice."

"You'd do that?"

Joyce shrugged. "In a heartbeat."

Abby didn't think Joshua would put his coffee

addiction ahead of his professional integrity. "How much does he rely on getting his coffee from you?"

"He drives in from the next town to get it and I supply him with coffee beans for the times when he can't make it in." Joyce pointed at the stack of journals on the table. "What are those?"

A dead end, Abby thought. So far, she hadn't come across any names that hadn't already been crossed off the list of suspects. Oddly, she hadn't seen any mention of Felicia's name. "I'm hoping Dermot might have written down something someone said that didn't make sense to him at the time."

The edge of Joyce's lip kicked up. "That would make the entire town eligible for an entry into his note-book. Hey, have you come across an entry for me?"

Abby was about to say no when she remembered seeing smiley faces next to the initials JB. "I think he liked you." She searched the journal and nodded. "Here we go. A bright happy face next to your initials. They're in every other page."

"How sweet, but why did he only put a smiley face on every other day?"

Abby didn't want to mention the bolt of lightning she'd seen on every other page. "Do you, by any chance, have a volatile temper?"

Joyce threw her hands up. "Ugh! Of course, I do. Who doesn't?"

When her lips stretched into a wide smile, Abby could have sworn the sun shone brightly out of her eyes.

"Okay, I guess today is a smiley day." She might make a point of steering clear of the café on the lightning bolt days. Although that would mean missing out on coffee. No point in leading a life without risks.

Joyce crossed her arms and shook her head. "I can't help feeling I might have missed something and I'm kicking myself for it. What if I saw the killer and didn't notice? That would make me an accomplice by default."

"I'm sure you can't be locked up for that. If it's any consolation, the day I arrived I bumped into someone. I know it was a woman but I wouldn't be able to describe her to you."

"Tall? Short? Skinny? Chubby? *Rubenesque*?"

"About my height." She'd worn a jacket. Abby remembered her adjusting it but she couldn't remember the color. "Older than me. I couldn't say by how much. I only have this vague feeling she might have been in her fifties." Abby clicked her fingers. "Now I have this fleeting sensation of haughtiness. I remember apologizing and sensing disapproval."

"Was she moving when you bumped into her?" Joyce asked.

"Yes." Abby sat forward. "And I think she might have been coming from Edgar Street, and we know that leads to Allan Street which leads to Poe Lane, but if I'm right, we'd have to get the snoopy neighbor to collaborate the sighting."

"I've been doing some reading about people who

153

use poison as their weapon," Joyce said. "They plan ahead."

True. Abby remembered having a similar thought the previous night.

"Killing someone with poison, by its very nature, requires careful planning and subterfuge," Joyce continued. "That means killers who use poison tend to be cunning, sneaky, and creative." Joyce leaned forward and lowered her voice. "They tend to avoid physical confrontation. Instead, they rely on verbal and emotional manipulation to get what they want."

"Are you about to suggest we should be looking for a woman?" Abby asked.

"It goes without saying. We should also focus on someone highly creative. They can design the murder plan in as much detail as if they were writing the script for a play."

Abby sat back and looked up at the ceiling. Faith had mentioned she belonged to a theatre group. "Do you happen to have someone in mind?"

"We have a group called the Eden Thespians. I'm going to make a list of all the members."

Abby smiled. "We can't start suspecting the entire town. That could get us into trouble and cause friction in the community."

Joyce shrugged. "Don't lower your guard. For all you know, I might have suggested the Eden Thespians as a way to get you off my back."

Another email came through on her cell phone.

Abby glanced at it but didn't open it. "These pancakes are exceptionally good. How do you get them so fluffy?"

"Easy. I just pin the order in the kitchen and magic happens." Joyce nudged her head toward the window. "I just saw Joshua drive by. He looked serious."

"You have a keen eye." Abby turned but she only caught sight of the car.

"He drove by slowly and appeared to be looking for someone." Joyce gave her a pointed look.

"I haven't done anything. Honestly."

"Maybe he found Doyle."

Abby set her fork down. "You all play it to the hilt." Abby thought Joyce would plead ignorance. Instead she gave a casual shrug.

"I told you we like to keep ourselves entertained. By the way, a bunch of us get together at the inn on Fridays for drinks and a movie night. Come along. This week we're watching The Great Gatsby. It'll be your first time so we'll forgive your inappropriate attire, but for future reference, we like to dress up."

"That sounds like a challenge."

"It's easy. We all make use of the Eden Thespian's wardrobe department."

Maybe she could use that as an excuse to prod them for information. "Where do I find these Eden Thespians?"

"Across the road in the Wilde building. Another coffee?" Joyce asked.

Abby gave a distracted nod.

"Your phone's ringing," Joyce said and got up to place her order.

Frowning, Abby looked at the caller ID. Her mom. And she wanted to video chat… Abby raked her fingers through her hair. Was she up to doing a face to face? "Mom. What a surprise."

"For a moment there I thought you weren't going to answer. Let me look at you. I've been so worried…"

"Why? I'm fine."

"You don't have a fixed address. Does that sound fine to you? Where are you? I want to see."

Abby held the cell phone up. "I'm here."

"And where exactly is here?"

"Joyce's café." Abby gave her mom a visual tour. "This is Joyce, the owner."

Joyce didn't need any encouragement. She smiled and waved and, setting the coffee down, she introduced herself.

"Call me Eleanor," her mom said.

Joyce gave her a bright smile. "You don't need to worry about Abby, Eleanor. We'll take good care of her. Eden is a safe little…"

Joyce's voice was drowned out by the sound of police sirens, but she continued speaking. "… She's met everyone and she already loves my coffee. Oh, and she has a dog. You'll love him."

"What was that?" Eleanor asked.

Joyce smiled. "That was our local law enforcement doing their job."

Her mom pressed her hand to her chest. "Does Eden have a high crime rate?"

The concern in her mom's voice made Abby cringe. Born and raised in Iowa, one of the safest states in which to live, she had worried about Abby moving to Seattle to work and had been almost catatonic when Abby had broken the news about moving half way around the world.

A children's book illustrator, she worked from home and had a morbid fear of flying. Also, after attending several weddings out-of-state, she had developed an intense dislike of long distance travel by car or train.

Mostly, she had an unreasonable attitude to the need to spread one's wings and see the world. In her mom's opinion you only needed to close your eyes and you could go anywhere and experience anything without leaving your home.

Whatever explanation Joyce had offered about the crime rate in Eden seemed to have done the trick. Her mom now sounded chatty.

"I'm glad to see you've settled in," her mom said. "Any idea what you'll do for a job? I hear your employer is dead."

"H-how did you... where—"

"It's called the international media, Abby. Has the killer been caught?"

"Not yet," Joyce said. "But we're working on it. Abby's been interrogating all the locals."

"That sounds dangerous," her mom said.

"She should be fine. Abby's already come face-to-face with our most dangerous local and she came through without a scrape. She's also trying to prove to the newspaper owner that we need a local paper."

Heaven help her, she'd never hear the end of it.

Abby drove for fifteen minutes before she spotted the farmhouse in the distance. The stretch of road leading out of town had been desolate for the most part; the only other driver she'd seen had chugged along in an old VW Beetle.

Doyle yawned and peered out the passenger window.

"Are we there yet? Is that what you're asking me?"

Felicia's farmhouse was set well back from the main road. She kept a couple of horses in the front paddock and some cows in the paddocks beyond the farmhouse.

Abby was about to turn into the long driveway when her cell phone rang. "Hello, detective. Just the person I wanted to speak with. We heard police sirens earlier on. Would you care to make a statement?"

"Nothing but a false alarm," he assured her.

Surprised that he'd given her even that much information, Abby smiled. "Joyce and I were in the middle of telling my mom I had moved to a quiet little town. Can you imagine what my mom thought when she heard the sirens?"

"I'm sorry about that. Would you like me to speak with her and offer assurances?" he asked.

"That might help." Abby tapped the steering wheel. "What exactly will you say to her?"

"That the little town of Eden had been incident free until you arrived."

Abby exchanged a raised eyebrow look with Doyle. "She'll insist I catch the first available flight back home. Would you care to revise your story?"

"Yes, I suppose."

A feeling of lightness swelled inside her. "So, what can I do for you, detective?"

"You could tell me where you are."

"Out and about, enjoying a drive."

"And staying out of trouble?"

"Of course. Anything else?"

"The tea caddies have been tested and were all free of cyanide."

Abby sat up. "You're willingly sharing information with me?"

"I thought it might be an effective way of keeping you out of trouble."

"Does this actually put anyone in the clear?" Abby asked.

"No. It just means the poison was put in the teapot," Joshua said. "Any thoughts?"

"I'll have to get back to you." She disconnected the call and turned into the driveway, keeping her eyes out for stray pets and livestock.

"If Felicia minds me driving in, I'm going to say I'm lost and wanted to ask for directions."

Doyle rolled his eyes.

"What? You don't think she'll buy that?" It took a couple of minutes for Doyle to climb out of the car. "Honestly, you're a worrywart and stubborn."

When her knock at the front door went unanswered, Abby suggested going around the back. "It's a large property. Felicia might be out and about... doing farm things like feeding the chickens."

A shed stood a few feet away from the house. When Abby strode toward it, Doyle whined. "What? She might be inside. You can't expect me to turn my nose up at an open invitation to snoop. I knocked at the front door and no one answered. We're out in the middle of nowhere. What if she twisted her ankle and needs assistance?" Doyle lowered his head. "Yeah, see. You didn't think of that. Did you know farming is one of the most dangerous occupations? Animals can inflict injuries. Bites. Kicks. Ramming. People can fall from ladders. Then there are the hazards of using machinery such as tractors. Vehicles can overturn." She eased the door open and stepped inside the shed. Neat shelves lined one side of the wall with labeled canisters and farm paraphernalia. "And let's not forget chemicals.

Pesticides and herbicides. They can all cause injuries such as burns, respiratory illness or... poisoning."

A sound behind her had her looking around.

Abby grimaced and whispered, "I guess you reserve the right to say I told you so." Abby stared at the rifle aimed straight at her.

Chapter Fifteen

"You're trespassing." The woman, who looked a great deal like Felicia Williams, held the rifle aimed straight at Abby.

"Put the gun down, Felicity."

Felicity and Felicia? Sisters, Abby assumed.

"She's that nosy reporter, Felicia, and we've caught her red-handed snooping around."

"I knocked on the front door but there was no answer," Abby said, her voice remarkably steady for someone who'd never had a weapon pointed at her. "I only want to ask some questions... for the face of the town series I'm writing."

"A likely story," Felicity bellowed. "You've been spreading gossip about Felicia. I don't understand why you've been cleared. You're the only one who was seen going into Dermot Cavendish's house that morning."

"How do you happen to know that?" Abby asked.

"It's common knowledge," Felicia said. "Everyone in town is talking about it."

"And how do you know that? Rumor has it, you never go into town," Abby said.

"I suggest you get back in your car and take off or else." Felicity adjusted her aim and made a clicking sound, which left Abby in no doubt. The woman was trigger-happy.

Felicia strode up to the gun-wielding woman and somehow managed to talk her into lowering her weapon. "You really should go."

"Last night you were full of questions about me. More than anyone else has asked. Now it's my turn," Abby said. "Where did you know Dermot from?"

Felicia's eyes hardened. "What's that got to do with that ridiculous article you're pretending to write?"

Abby shrugged. "Everyone has been happy to talk about him. It helps with the mourning process." Something flickered in Felicia's eyes. For a brief moment they appeared to soften.

As the two women had a whispered conversation Abby looked down at Doyle and gave him a reassuring smile. "I'm sure they'll come to their senses," she whispered.

"All right," Felicia said. "You can come in."

Doyle huffed out a breath. "What?" Abby whispered. "You think it's a bad idea?" She supposed Joshua would think so too. In fact, she didn't look forward to him finding out about her visit to the farm.

She followed the two women inside the house, while Doyle trailed a couple of steps behind her.

Felicia showed her through to a sitting room and gestured for her to sit down.

Large bay windows offered a view of the mountains and the surrounding countryside. The room was elegantly furnished in a city meets country chic style. No expense spared, Abby thought admiring the table lamps. The chair she sat on certainly didn't sink and the cushion was nice and plump.

Cool colors prevailed. Mostly ice blues and neutral shades of gray. The decorator, Abby thought, had added subtle echoes of the surrounding countryside with a few rustic pieces scattered around the stone fireplace, including a collection of box picture frames displaying rusty nails. The lace curtains were gathered with an ice blue sash. Abby decided Felicia liked the color blue...

She frowned and remembered the first day when she'd arrived she'd made her way to Dermot's house and had bumped into a woman. A woman wearing a light blue jacket. Could that have been Felicia coming from Dermot's house?

Felicia gave the sleeve of her jacket a tug. "Would you like a cup of tea?"

While Abby was curious to see her crockery set, she declined. "I'm more of a coffee drinker and I've already had some, thank you for offering." Turning to Felicity, she gave her a small smile. "That's a serious looking weapon."

"This is my sister Felicity. She's visiting. As for the rifle, I live alone and it's isolated out here," Felicia offered.

Abby didn't think she'd ever met such unhappy looking people. Both had thin downturned mouths and what appeared to be perpetual scowls. She wondered if they'd met Bartholomew Carr...

"This is a nice spread you have here," Abby said.

"I worked hard for it," Felicia snapped, her tone defensive.

Meaning what? She'd earned every penny herself and had purchased the property outright with no financial assistance?

Abby looked down at Felicia's hands and didn't see a wedding band or any telltale signs of her ever having worn one. She had an aunt who was divorced and even after a dozen years she still had the habit of rubbing her wedding ring finger.

"I really am writing an article about the folk who live in Eden," Abby offered.

"Why?"

Good question, Abby thought. "It's a way of celebrating people who might otherwise fade into the background."

"What exactly is the point? Do you want to be the feel-good fairy?"

"I believe everyone has a story to tell and we can all benefit from hearing them. Especially today's youth."

Felicia rolled her eyes. "Everyone knows everyone's

business here so I doubt you'll be able to scrape up anything new. Admit it, this is nothing but a way for you to get people to like you."

Felicia had insinuated as much the night before at the pub. Did she have an issue with that? "Where do you stand on the Lamington saga?" The question earned Abby another roll of the eyes. Abby leaned forward. "I get the feeling you have a low opinion of people."

"I came out here to enjoy some peace and quiet."

Something she surely got since she didn't seem to be the slightest bit interested in mixing with anyone. "How did you choose this place?"

Felicia's cheeks colored slightly. "I hired someone to find me the most suitable house in the area."

Yes, but... Why here? "Did you maybe want to be closer to someone?" it occurred to ask.

Felicia lifted her chin. "That's none of your business."

"Even if you think you've led a private life and covered your tracks, there are ways of finding out." Abby shifted to the edge of her seat. "Last night was not the first time we met. The day Dermot died, I saw you coming from the general direction of his house. I'm willing to bet anything you went to see him that day."

Felicity jumped to her feet and cocked her rifle. "Right, that's it. Interview over. Now get out."

"Oh, I'm sorry. Did I hit a nerve?"

When Abby returned to town, she headed straight for the Gazette. Faith had put up a sign saying she'd gone on a break but had left the door open. Deciding to wait for her, Abby settled at a desk and drew out her cell phone. "Good time to catch up on that email." She'd only skimmed it, but it had been enough to get an idea of what her ex-boss was offering her.

The email had an attachment. A contract.

Checking to see if Faith's computer was password protected, she forwarded the attachment and opened it to print out. If anything, it would serve as a reminder that she still had options. Reading the email again, she realized her ex-boss simply assumed she would jump at the chance to return to her old job.

"He's in for a rude awakening." She'd most likely turn down the offer, although, it wouldn't do to burn her bridges. Leaning back, she looked out the window. Would she change her mind and take him up on the offer?

Doyle woofed lightly seconds before Faith strode in and laughed. "Hello to you too." Turning to Abby she smiled. "Good to see you came back in one piece. I was just over at the café and Joyce mentioned you were going to pay Felicia Williams a visit."

"Yes, well... That was my bit of excitement for the day." Abby told her about snooping around the shed and being caught in the act.

"Hey, what's this? Did you bring me cake?" Faith asked.

"No, I didn't." A box sat on the counter and if Abby had noticed it, she hadn't paid much attention to it.

"Oh, I know what this is. Lamingtons. It's a blind taste. Everyone entering the contest submits a platter and we always get a box. Dermot used to get me to eat them and give him my opinion."

"Was he a judge?"

"Everyone takes turns. There's an official panel of judges and they always invite someone from the town to even things out a bit. Dermot took part in it last year but he didn't feel comfortable about it because he didn't eat cake."

"So how did he do the judging?"

"He nibbled while everyone else scoffed theirs. Here, have one."

The little squares looked delectable. Joyce had described them as sponge cake covered in a chocolate sauce and desiccated coconut. Taking a bite of one, she chewed.

"Well?"

"Light. Moist. Not as sweet as I thought it would be. I've had something similar to this. Coconut bars."

"Similar but surely not the same."

Abby helped herself to another one. "Oh, this one has a strawberry jam filling."

Faith licked some coconut off her fingers. "I wonder if Hanna entered the competition this year. She'll win hands down."

Doyle whimpered. "Sorry, Doyle. It has chocolate

and even I know doggies are not supposed to eat chocolate." Abby licked her fingers and considered tasting another one.

"One more won't kill you," Faith said and polished off her second one.

Abby peered inside the box. "Is there a rule about size?"

"Yes. It helps to keep the competition fair and the contest participants anonymous. Although, some are a dead giveaway. I've had Agnes Newman's Lamingtons so I know she's the only one who prefers to use apricot jam in hers. Last year there was a huge debate about excluding anything that didn't adhere to the traditional plain Lamingtons."

"Why not introduce different categories?" Abby asked.

"That would make sense, but any change has to be submitted to the committee and approved by them." Faith rolled her eyes. "They're not known for their flexibility. I've seen them carrying tape measures to make sure everyone sticks to the rules. They can be scary."

Smiling, Abby bit into another Lamington. Her reflexes kicked in and she spat it out. "Ugh."

Doyle lunged for the morsel Abby had spat out. "No, Doyle. Leave it." Abby made a grab for him.

"I guess that one didn't taste so good," Faith remarked.

Abby grimaced and, still holding Doyle, rushed to the sink to rinse her mouth. "I've never tasted anything so foul. I've had the misfortune of cracking an egg and finding it rotten inside. I cannot begin to tell you how bad that smells. This matches it in taste. Do you have a mint?"

"I have toothpaste and a stash of toothbrushes."

Abby followed her to the back room. "My mouth feels numb." She brushed and rinsed and brushed and rinsed again. She then gargled and began the process again. "Ugh. That was dreadful."

Faith handed her a bottle of water. "Did you swallow any of it?"

"No." She grabbed a paper tissue and wiped the cake she'd spat out off the floor.

"Don't throw it out. The police might want to test it," Faith said as she picked up the phone to call the police. When she finished, she dialed again. "I'm calling the Lamington Committee." Moments later, Faith finished the call and frowned. "This is strange. They haven't actually made any deliveries. In fact, they're running late with their sample boxes and had planned on doing it tomorrow."

"So where did that box come from?" Abby asked.

"You said it was here when you arrived. Someone must have dropped it off when I stepped out for a break."

Abby tipped the bottle of water back and drank deeply. Moments later, Joshua arrived and found them both staring at the box of Lamingtons.

"Someone tried to poison Abby," Faith said.

Abby hugged Doyle against her chest. "We can't be sure of that. The box was delivered here, so you might have been the target."

Faith screeched. "Me?"

After a lengthy discussion, they decided Abby had been the most likely target probably because word had spread about her writing an article about the ongoing Lamington saga.

She turned to the detective. "I remember telling you about it. Have you been talking about me?"

"Do I look like I spread gossip around?" the detective asked. "Maybe someone at the café overheard you." He took the box away for testing and promised to get back to her with the results as soon as they came in.

"If I hadn't just come from Felicia Williams' house, I'd think she'd had something to do with poisoning the Lamingtons."

"Would you like me to see what I can find out about her?" Faith offered. We already know she worked as a chemist. She'd know all about poisons. If we can find a connection to Dermot, it might bring us closer to a motive for maybe wanting to poison you."

"Okay. You work on that. Meanwhile, I need some fresh air. Also, I'm going to return Dermot's journals and finally drop in on June Laurie."

Chapter Sixteen

*W*hen Abby reached number 12 Edgar Street and knocked on the door she hoped no one would answer. She felt fine but the idea of someone trying to poison her had left her feeling shaken.

Did someone feel threatened by her? She tried to think what might have triggered such a violent reprisal but came up empty.

If only one or several Lamingtons had been poisoned, the killer had gone to a lot of trouble to put together the contents of the box, making sure to include a variety to give the impression they had come from various sources.

She knocked again and as she waited, she checked her cell phone. Joshua had promised to contact her as soon as he had some results but she doubted that would happen any time soon.

After the third knock, she decided to give up, which was just as well because she'd had no idea what she would ask June. The cleaning lady had already been questioned a couple of times by Joshua and had obviously been cleared of any involvement.

Doyle trotted beside her, his nose in the air as if sniffing out any sign of trouble. She hoped that didn't mean anything. "I refuse to believe someone tried to poison me. It must have just been a bad Lamington. Why do I think that? Well, the person who sent the cakes wouldn't have any way of making sure only I ate them. And I seriously doubt anyone would want Faith to fall ill... or worse." Perhaps it had been a warning to stay away and stop snooping around. After all, the first bite had been enough to put her on the alert. The reminder made her gag.

They reached Dermot's house and, using the key Sebastian had given her, Abby let herself in. She put the journals back and had a quick look around the study.

Doyle whined softly. "In a hurry to get somewhere?" Abby asked. He woofed and scurried to the study door. "I won't be long. I just want to make sure I haven't missed something obvious."

Doyle woofed again. "What is it, Doyle?" A feeling of apprehension had her tensing. Abby turned around, or at least, she tried to. When her body eventually responded, she looked toward the door where Doyle stood at attention, his soft growl breaking the silence in the house.

"Doyle?" Abby whispered. She inched toward him. Had she heard a floorboard creak? Yes. Definitely. There was someone else in the house. Sebastian?

As far as she knew, no one else had the keys to the house. No one, except... "June Laurie," Abby whispered and tried to get up the courage to peer down the hallway. She looked down at Doyle and caught him looking up at her, his expression a mixture of amusement and puzzlement, Abby thought.

Doyle took a tentative step forward and peered down the hallway.

"What do you see?"

He looked up at Abby and then took another step.

"I guess that means the coast is clear." Scooping in a breath, she followed Doyle down the hallway, crouching down with each step she took. Thinking she'd heard another noise, she stopped in mid-step. Doyle lowered his head and sniffed the floor. A few more steps brought them up to the kitchen.

She figured the only way to do this was to take the plunge. "On the count of three," she mouthed. In that split second, she threw all caution to the winds and leaped forward, only to shriek in response to the other person's shriek.

While Abby sprung back, the other person lunged at her with a rolling pin.

Doyle found his voice and fired out a series of barks.

Abby and the rolling pin wielding woman looked down at him, their eyes registering surprise.

"Good boy, Doyle." Abby looked the woman square in the eye. "He bites and I have no way of controlling him, so I suggest you put down your weapon."

"You're that reporter."

Felicity had used the same accusatory tone. What was up with that? Abby nodded. "Do you have a problem with that?" The woman wore a housecoat and a headscarf. "June? June Laurie?"

The woman lifted her chin. "Yes."

"What are you doing here?"

"My job."

"A likely story. Everyone knows you come in early."

"Only because that's the way Dermot liked it. Now that he's gone, I thought I'd come in and give the place a thorough clean. I have Sebastian Cavendish's permission."

"Oh, I see."

June gave her a lifted eyebrow look. "So, what are you doing in here?"

Abby held up the house key. "I too have Sebastian's permission."

They both lowered their shoulders.

"Right... well... I thought you might have been the killer returning to the scene of the crime," June said. "They always do that on TV."

Abby didn't want to admit she should have entertained the same thought. After the close encounter she'd had with the Lamington, she should have kept her guard up. Instead, she'd been fixated about finding something... anything she might have missed. Abby gaped.

"What?" June asked.

She'd just realized something. "Sorry, I just had a stray thought about Dermot's journals. He'd mentioned everyone he ever encountered, but there is one name missing." Felicia's name. There hadn't been a single mention of her. She'd noticed it before but now the information swirled around her mind as if trying to prompt her into attaching some significance to it.

Dermot hadn't cared much for his snoopy neighbor, Thelma Harrison. Yet, there had been regular mentions of her. Nothing derogatory. Just general remarks. Thelma looked cheerful today. Thelma's had her hair done.

"Well? Are you going to tell me?" June asked.

"Do you remember Dermot ever mentioning Felicia Williams?"

"That stuck up old stick?" June shook her head. "There's a photo of her on the mantle. She's glaring at Dermot for no good reason. I mentioned it to him once. Told him there was something odd about her and Dermot said some people just wanted to be left alone and didn't care to socialize. As for the way she's looking at him, he said none of us got to pick and choose how we looked so we shouldn't judge."

"Did he know her from somewhere?"

"I got the feeling he did but he never said anything."

When Doyle barked again, Abby lifted her

eyebrows. "I'd no idea you were such a good guard dog. What is it, Doyle?"

He trotted over to the back door.

"Oh, he probably heard my Henry."

"Your Henry?"

"My husband is sitting outside waiting for me to finish. I told him I needed to clean today and he wouldn't let me come here alone. He's been trying to talk me into quitting my job, but what would I do with myself?" She glanced at Abby. "I know what you must be thinking. A cleaning lady attached to her job? Well, cleaning people's house is an honest job. My mother did it. My grandmother did it. I have a daughter who put herself through school cleaning people's houses. I offered to pay for her studies but she refused saying cleaning gave her time to think."

For some reason, Abby felt chastised. "I've always done my own cleaning," she felt compelled to say. "Did you ever cook for Dermot?"

June shook her head. "That's one domestic task I never cared for. Henry and I enjoy eating out at the pub. It's a good way to round up our day. Their food is just like home cooking."

"So you don't have an entry for the Lamington contest?"

June laughed. "I get my fill of cakes every weekend and there's always a Lamington drive."

"What's that?"

"The local school organizes all the parents to bake

Lamingtons and they're sold to raise money for the school." June set down the rolling pin. "My Henry must be getting restless. I should get going."

"Lovely to meet you at last, June."

June nodded and, taking her apron off, she trotted off.

"We can at least cross her off the list." Abby pressed her hand to her chest. "That was too much excitement for me." She sank down on a chair and wondered what to do next. Stretching her legs out, she looked out the window.

"Everyone we thought had a reason to want to see Dermot dead has been cleared." She checked her cell phone for messages even though she knew it would be too soon to hear back from the lab. "Can you believe someone might have tried to poison me?"

Doyle shook his head. When he scratched his ear, Abby decided he hadn't actually been answering her.

On a whim, she decided to call Joshua and tell him about June Laurie. The moment he answered, she forgot about June Laurie and actually said, "I need you to tell me if the police has linked the deaths which have been reported recently." She'd been focusing on finding a killer among the locals, but what if Dermot had fallen prey to a serial killer roaming the countryside?

"Yes."

"Pardon? Did I hear you correctly?"

"I was about to call you. You're bound to read all about it in the morning edition," Joshua said. "The deaths are linked to each other but not to Dermot's death. The victims all died from rat poisoning and the person responsible has been apprehended."

"Well, that's a relief." Abby sat up. "What was his motive?"

"Revenge. Years before he and the victims had belonged to a motorcycle gang. The police raided their headquarters and busted them for drug trafficking. The victims set him up as the fall guy. After serving his time, he was released. Instead of enjoying his freedom, he decided to go on a killing spree and get revenge on everyone who'd betrayed him."

Abby chortled. "I don't suppose he used Lamingtons to deliver the poison?" She waited for Joshua to respond. First came the long exhalation. That was followed by some throat clearing. "Detective?"

"Short answer. No. He didn't use Lamingtons to deliver the poison. However…"

Abby raked her fingers through her hair. "You're drawing this out. Why?"

"It's rather a delicate matter."

"Someone trying to poison me? Yeah, I'll say it is. Did I step on someone's toes?"

"No. After his release, the killer made his way to his elderly aunt's house. He's in his fifties and his aunt is in her early eighties and suffering from bouts of dementia."

"That's unfortunate."

"In more ways than one. She actually lives nearby

and every year, she enjoys entering the Lamington contest. This year was no exception. As she's getting on in age, she rather hoped she'd win a ribbon before she... runs out of time."

Abby cupped her chin in her hand. "She sounds sweet... despite her unfortunate relationship with a killer."

"Yes. That's why we're treating this with... kid gloves. She is sweet and she had nothing to do with her nephew's criminal activities. You have to understand, this was an accident."

"What was an accident?"

"Mistaking the sugar she needed for the last batch of Lamingtons she baked with the rat poison her nephew had stored in a canister."

Abby heard the hallway clock tick.

"Abby? Are you still there?"

"Yes," she replied in a small voice. Abby sat up. "Wait a minute. The box contained a variety of Lamingtons."

"That's right. As I said, she's been trying to win a ribbon for quite some time. This year, she decided to enter every single flavor she could think of. Sending them to the Gazette was her way of trying to impress at least one of the judges. I should add, she didn't know about Dermot's death. Like I said, she's not well and some days, she doesn't quite know what's what."

"I see." Abby slumped back on the chair. "What's her name?"

"Ah... well. This is the part where we're doing our best to spare her further humiliation. We've decided to withhold her name. You have to understand, she didn't do it on purpose."

Abby's voice hitched. "You think I'd press charges?"

"No. I mean, I don't think you would. She has a health care worker looking after her, but when her nephew appeared on the scene, he sent her away. Now she's back and assures us this will never happen again."

Abby sighed. "Well, at least that's one mystery solved." She took a moment to enjoy the feeling of relief. She hadn't been a target. Although, she had come close to becoming a statistic. Abby looked down at Doyle. "That's a sort of wake-up call. Enjoy every moment because you never know what's around the corner. I think this calls for a celebratory cup of coffee."

Chapter Seventeen

"There is one person I haven't spoken with. Thelma Harrison." Doyle gave her a wide-eyed look. "You think that's asking for trouble? It would be remiss of me to exclude her. After all, she is the one and only eyewitness." The eyewitness who'd failed to see the killer entering Dermot's house.

Doyle whimpered.

"Is that a warning or are you just telling me we've done enough for today and should head back home?" Abby locked the front door and stepped out. Expecting to see Thelma peering at her from the window, she looked across the lane.

"Well, if she's been keeping tabs on the place she sure is doing a fine job of staying out of sight." Abby crossed the narrow lane and knocked on Thelma's door.

While she waited, she turned and looked over at Dermot's house. Thelma had an uninterrupted view of his front door and the lane was narrow. She'd be able to both see and hear anyone approaching.

The door opened but only enough for Abby to see a light blue eye and part of a pale cheek.

"Can I help you?" a thin voice asked.

Abby introduced herself. "I've been meaning to drop by and say hello."

The door opened another fraction. "You're that reporter who's been dropping in to visit Sebastian Cavendish."

Abby nodded and before she could ask if she could have a word with her, Thelma opened the door and beckoned her inside.

Thelma wore a hounds-tooth patterned suit. Abby couldn't be sure, but she suspected it might be an original Coco Chanel suit. Thelma was probably in her late seventies or early eighties; old enough to have been around when the suits had been the height of fashion.

The narrow hallway, painted in a light beige tone, was lit by an old-fashioned carriage light.

"Come through." Thelma invited her through to the sitting room lusciously furnished in a Parisian style with art deco pieces displayed on the mantelpiece and on small side tables.

From the outside, Abby would never have guessed the house would be furnished so elegantly. Thelma gestured toward a settee while she made herself comfortable on a royal blue club chair.

Doyle sat by Abby's feet, his manners impeccable.

Abby remarked on the lovely room as she took in the black and white photographs covering an entire wall.

"I traveled extensively," Thelma explained. "Charles, my late husband, came from money. Our first trip to Europe was by sea." She pointed at a photo of a young couple sitting at a sidewalk café. "That's us at *Les Deux Magot* café in Paris. We always made a point of going there at least once during our stays in Paris. When I married him, he'd worked as a lawyer but then he became a judge." Thelma shivered slightly. "He used to tell me about his cases. I could never understand the horrors people could inflict on others. Luckily, Charles passed away in his sleep. When I lost him, my interest in traveling faded and I came to live here."

Abby marveled at the choices people made. Thelma had lived in the city and had enjoyed all the distractions the city had to offer. What had brought her to a small town?

"This house had belonged to my grandparents. It's quite modest, but to them it was always a castle. When I came here to settle the estate I fell in love with... the town."

Thelma's chattiness struck Abby as odd. She came across as someone eager to share her experiences but reluctant to step out of the house. She wondered if it had something to do with a phobia. Then she remembered either Joyce or Faith saying Thelma usually went out for lunch.

"Do you remember ever seeing this woman visiting

Dermot?" Abby asked as she showed her the photograph of Felicia Williams.

Thelma studied the picture for some time and finally shook her head. "He always received visitors. Every afternoon, they visited him for tea and a chat. When I first moved here, he invited me but I... I turned him down. Then he never invited me again."

Abby tried to pick up on any feeling of resentment but she only sensed resignation.

Thelma whispered, "I think he should have..."

"Pardon?"

Thelma looked at her with vacant eyes.

Out of curiosity, Abby asked her if June Laurie used the front door to let herself in to Dermot's house.

"The front door," Thelma said. "Why do you ask?"

Yet earlier, June had gone out the back door. "We've been trying to piece together a time frame of events listing everyone who came to see him the day he died."

Thelma nodded and, checking her watch, she slid to the edge of her chair.

The hallway clock struck the hour.

"I'm sure the police have already asked you to provide any information that might come to you..."

"They have. I'm sorry to say, I don't have anything else to add."

Abby thanked Thelma Harrison for her time and left. "Let's swing by the Gazette and then go back to the pub. We need to tell Faith about the poisoned Lamington."

She found Faith busy at her computer; her lips

pressed together, her brows furrowed. "Sorry to break your concentration."

"It's fine. I've been tracking down Felicia's career, but so far, I haven't found anything to connect her to Dermot. Not directly."

Abby noticed something odd about Faith. It took her a moment to put her finger on it. Faith always smiled, but not now. "Are you all right?"

"Yeah, sure. Why wouldn't I be?" Faith pushed back from her desk and huffed out a breath. "Actually, no. I'm not all right." She picked up a piece of paper and waved it at Abby. "You left this behind."

"What?"

"A contract. I'm guessing you've been offered your old job back."

"Oh."

"Oh? Is that all you have to say for yourself? When were you going to tell me? Or were you going to leave without so much as a goodbye?"

"I... I wouldn't do that."

"I get that you might not even have a job here, but you could at least wait until Sebastian makes up his mind. This is a lovely town. We have a lot to offer. I'm sure you have friends and family back home, but here..." Faith visibly swallowed. "Forget I said anything. I'm... I'm not any good with sudden changes and I've had more than my share this week." Faith slumped down. "I'm... I'm going to be sorry to see you go. And what will happen to Doyle?"

Doyle pricked up his ears and whined.

"Faith, you're scaring Doyle."

"Sorry, I shouldn't have said anything. Clearly, we can't compete with a big city newspaper."

Abby sighed. "If you must know, I hadn't even given it any thought. I only printed that out because I needed to hold it in my hands." Abby shrugged. "Coming here took a lot of courage. I know I was lucky to be offered this job. The timing—" She stooped down and gave Doyle a scratch under his chin. "It's a long story and I've put it all behind me."

"But now you're over whatever happened and you're ready to go back?" Faith asked.

Abby gave a slow shake of her head. "I'm not sure. I don't think so."

"I guess you want time to think about it."

Abby nodded.

"And I guess that'll have to do for now." Faith gave her a wobbly smile and turned to her computer screen. "Remember I told you I'd catalogued everything in the office? Well, Dermot kept copies of every editorial he wrote. About twenty years ago, he was involved in an investigative piece and was responsible for uncovering a scam at a chemical plant. They were dumping toxic waste straight into the river. Anyhow, Dermot got all his information from a whistle blower."

The whistle blower's identity remained protected, Faith went on to say, but according to her research

Felicia Williams had worked at that chemical plant during the time of the cover-up.

"You think she was the whistle blower?" Abby asked.

"There's only one way to find out. You'll have to ask her."

Abby put it at the top of her to-do list for the next day. "I think we've done enough for today. How about we go grab a coffee," Abby suggested.

As they made their way to Joyce's Café, Abby told Faith about the poisoned Lamington and her encounter with June Laurie. "Doyle is actually a great guard dog." He looked up at her and gave her a doggie grin.

Faith sighed. "You should at least come to our movie night. We'll either throw you a farewell party or give you a proper welcome by inducting you into our girls' movie night club."

Abby wished she could put her at ease, but if push came to shove, she'd have to be practical. After all, she too had bills to pay.

The café was doing its usual brisk business but they managed to get a table. Moments later, Joyce joined them.

"I hear you might be leaving us," Joyce said.

Abby looked at Faith who shrugged. "Sorry. When I saw the contract, I felt bereft and had to talk to someone so I called Joyce and she told me not to jump to conclusions."

"I've already told everyone you're coming to our

movie night," Joyce said. "Am I going to have to call them all again and say you've changed your mind?"

"That depends," Abby said, the edge of her lip lifting.

Joyce's neat eyebrows curved slightly. "On?"

"What movie we're watching."

Joyce gave her a nod of approval. "I already told you, it's The Great Gatsby."

"Then I'll be there."

"Good, that's settled. Now, what will you have?"

"An Easy Rider espresso, please."

"Cake?"

"No thanks. I had Lamingtons earlier, and I'm happy to say I survived to tell the tale."

Faith checked her watch. "I'll have the same. We have Dermot's wake to go to."

As they drunk their coffees they watched a parade of people streaming toward the pub.

"It's already started," Joyce said. "Everyone wants a chance to go into the pub and pay their respects. I suspect it's going to be a long night." She turned to Faith. "Have you picked a costume for our movie night?"

Faith nodded. "I found the most dazzling beaded dress complete with a headband. I'm coming as a flapper."

"I'm bringing a couple of bottles of champagne so we can have a proper toast to Dermot."

Faith rubbed her hands. "Joyce has excellent taste in

champagne and is quite extravagant. What are we drinking?"

"It's a special night. *Perrier Jouët Belle Époque*. I raided Mitch's cellar and he let me have them at cost."

Faith smiled at Abby. "We might live in the sticks, but we still indulge in fine French champagne."

"What should I bring?" Abby asked.

"Yourself and Doyle." Joyce got up to place their orders. "You can't leave him behind."

Abby worried her bottom lip. "Does he have to dress up too?"

"You could get him a little bow tie," Faith suggested. "That might look cute on him."

Abby caught sight of Doyle's eyebrows quirking up and laughed. "I swear he understands everything we say."

"Of course, he does. He's a smart doggie and one of the main reasons why you should stay."

"Really? The expensive French champagne already did the trick!" It would be good to kick back and relax, meet some new people, watch a movie...

"It's packed to the rafter," Faith said as they made their way inside the pub. People had spilled out onto the sidewalk and beyond. "This is turning into a street party. Dermot would have loved it."

"He was certainly admired by everyone." Abby saw

Mitch weaving his way around people to serve drinks. She then caught sight of a mop of red hair in the far corner and assumed that was his sister, Eddie. Markus had staked his place by the fireplace and looked more animated than Abby had seen him since arriving. It seemed everyone had a story to tell about Dermot.

"There's Sebastian," Faith pointed toward the bar.

Abby hugged Doyle against her chest. She wouldn't put him down for fear he might be trampled on.

As she moved through the crowd, Abby couldn't help being surprised at the number of people who smiled and acknowledged her. In reality, she'd only been living in the town for a few short days, but as Faith had said, she'd made a splash from the start.

When she reached the bar, the one person she hadn't expected to find there made eye contact with her.

Felicia Williams.

She stood a couple of feet away at the end of the bar with her sister beside her. Dressed in a powder blue jacket with her neat bob tucked back, Abby thought she resembled the film star, Lauren Bacall, albeit, an unhappy one. She really should do something about her downturned mouth, Abby couldn't help thinking as she gave the woman a nod of acknowledgment.

Abby couldn't understand why she'd come into town. Felicia wouldn't care what people thought of her, so she wouldn't feel pressured into publicly acknowledging Dermot's death.

Most people attended funerals and wakes out of

respect for the deceased and their family. Some found comfort in being with other mourners, sharing their loss, exchanging anecdotes...

Had Felicia's hard exterior crumbled? Despite the dim light in the pub, Abby could see her eyes looked slightly puffy as if from lack of sleep. She couldn't approach her again. Couldn't press her for more information. Not today.

Abby frowned. This really didn't make sense... and then, suddenly, it did.

Abby searched for Faith but couldn't see her anywhere. Faith had said Dermot had been old-fashioned and had never discussed his personal relationships. He'd talked about other people without any qualms, he'd mentioned them in his journals and, according to Faith, Dermot had talked to everyone. Everyone except Felicia Williams. At least not in public. Abby imagined this had been her choice, because she valued her privacy and had come here for peace and quiet.

Dermot had never mentioned her in his journals, and now Faith had found a possible connection between them. Had Felicia Williams been the whistle blower at the chemical plant she'd worked at. Had Faith found the missing link?

The more Abby thought about it, the more convinced she became. Dermot had met Felicia years before. That didn't bring Abby any closer to finding the killer but it unraveled the mystery of why Dermot had never mentioned Felicia.

Turning, she saw Joshua entering the pub. He waved to her. She waved back and they both shared a moment of indecision, their shoulders lifting and dropping. Abby laughed as they both began simultaneously moving toward each other.

A thought swept through her, but then Joshua spoke and she lost the thread...

"Quite a turnout," the detective said and gave Doyle a scratch under his chin.

"This might sound odd, but I feel privileged to be here." A feeling of deep regret rose inside her. She wished she'd had the opportunity to become better acquainted with Dermot.

Joshua nudged her arm and guided her toward the main entrance. "How are you feeling?" he asked as they stepped outside. "Are you experiencing any residual effects from the Lamington?"

"Thank goodness, no. Although I might give them a miss for a while." She set Doyle down and remembering her visit to Thelma, she told him about it. "I could never have imagined someone like her living in this small town. Eccentric comes to mind." And perhaps a little lonesome. "I can't decide if she misses her old life or if she's happy reminiscing. Her life has shrunk from traveling and seeing the world to sitting by the window and staring at—" Abby looked down the street.

"You've just had a sparkly idea."

Abby gave a small nod but didn't reply. There were too many thoughts weaving around her mind.

Thelma had come here to settle her grandparents' estate and then she'd decided to make Eden her home. Both she and Felicia enjoyed their privacy. What else did they have in common?

Abby told Joshua about the connection Faith had made between Dermot and Felicia.

"Does that mean you suspect her?" he asked.

"No, but from the start I asked Faith about the special people in Dermot's life. According to Faith, Dermot had been discreet. If he'd been having an affair with Felicia, no one would have known about it." Abby hitched her thumb over her shoulder. "She's inside. Why would someone who insists on keeping herself apart from everyone suddenly want to join in?" Abby frowned. "He should have asked again…"

"Who?"

"Sorry, my mind is racing. That's what Thelma whispered. He should have asked again. When she first arrived here Dermot invited her over for a drink and she turned him down. Now she regrets it… or maybe she's been regretting it all this time." Abby looked down at Doyle. "Come on, boy." She took off at a trot.

"Where are we going?" Joshua asked. "Hey, wait."

"All this time I've kept saying Thelma Harrison only saw me going inside Dermot's house. How could someone intent on keeping a vigil on Poe Lane have missed seeing the killer?"

"What are you saying?"

"There's definitely something Thelma is not telling us." He should have asked again, Abby thought. "Thelma told me she fell in love with the town."

"What's wrong with that?" Joshua asked.

"The pregnant pause before she specified she'd fallen in love with the town." They turned into Poe Lane and slowed their steps. "Do you hear that?"

"Music."

"It's the same music I heard playing at Dermot's house."

As Joshua knocked on the front door, Abby peered in through the window and gasped.

"What?"

Abby couldn't answer so she tugged his arm and pointed at the window.

"Oh hell," he said. The detective acted quickly, calling for police backup and emergency services.

Seeing him about to break the door down, Abby screeched. "No."

"Why?"

"Didn't you see the teapot next to her?"

"What about it?" It took a second for the meaning to sink in.

Abby nodded. "She's committed suicide. You can't go in there. There'll be fumes."

"But what if she's still alive?"

The soundtrack finished. They both stared at each other.

Growling under his breath, Joshua picked up a garden rock and, telling Abby to stand back, threw it at the window. Glass shattered as he rushed toward the door and slammed into it.

Abby didn't think the broken window would be enough to clear the room of all fumes.

It took a couple of tries but the old door hinges finally gave way and the door slammed open, but it was already too late.

Epilogue

*A*bby slumped down on the bed and stared at her suitcase. Doyle came to sit beside her. "I can't spend the rest of my life living out of a suitcase. She kicked the lid closed. "How do you feel about calling the pub home for a while longer?"

Doyle gave her a doggie grin and wagged his tail.

"Come on. Let's go to the Gazette. Faith will want to know we're staying."

Striding into the small-town newspaper, Abby drew in a deep breath and smiled. The office was a flurry of activity with the phone ringing and people coming in to get their free copy of the Gazette.

Faith emerged from behind her computer. "Oh, good. You're here." She tapped her watch. "And you're late. I've been up since the crack of dawn trying to get this week's edition out. By the way, thanks for sending in your piece. Dermot would have approved."

Her piece! An essay about community spirit and her impressions of the town. Writing it had helped her get through the night.

After finding Thelma Harrison dead, Abby had sat on the curb to watch while emergency services took over. A couple of men wearing breathing apparatus had gone in to retrieve the body. Joshua had stood by liaising with the police and organizing the clean-up.

A note had been found. Thelma Harrison's confession.

That fatal morning, Thelma had waited for June Laurie to leave the house and had decided to finally pay Dermot a visit. Thelma Harrison had spent years pining for him and regretting her decision to turn down his invitation. She'd spent years watching all those women coming and going, visiting Dermot for afternoon tea. Finally, she'd had enough and had decided to put an end to her misery... by killing Dermot.

Unable to live with what she'd done, she had decided to join him. If Thelma had survived, she would have been able to plead temporary insanity. In the note, she'd rambled on about all the ghastly stories her husband had told her about his murder cases. She'd thought Dermot had deserved a quicker death doing what he loved doing. Drinking tea.

Abby remembered wondering how Dermot could have drunk a poisoned cup of tea and had come up with the theory that he might have been groggy from inhaling the fumes.

She'd been right.

Thelma had snuck inside the house and had poured the poison in the teapot. Stepping back and watching from the safety of the hallway, she'd waited to see Dermot settling down on his chair and pouring himself a cup of tea. When she'd seen him slumping back, she'd rushed into the sitting room and had put on the music she'd heard playing the first time she'd seen him...

It had been a crime of passion, after all. Albeit, warped passion.

Word had spread and everyone attending the wake had made their way to Poe Lane. At one point, Abby had looked up and, seeing Felicia Williams, she'd made a beeline for her.

"You found him dead before I did," Abby had said. That first day when she'd made her way to Dermot's house, she'd bumped into someone. She'd guessed it had been Felicia.

Felicia Williams had nodded, going on to explain how she'd decided to finally visit Dermot and tell him she wanted their relationship to come out in the open. They had met years before when she'd provided him with vital inside information about the company she'd worked for. They'd been happy and he'd asked her to marry him, but she'd been far too independent and hadn't seen the need to tie herself down to marriage.

When Dermot had retired and moved to Eden permanently, Felicia had followed, at first spending weekends at a farm she'd purchased and then, finally moving here to be closer to him. To her chagrin, she'd insisted on maintaining their relationship a secret.

That morning, when she'd found him dead, she'd been distraught and had fled the house. She knew she should have called the police but explained that by the time she'd reached her car, she'd heard the police sirens and had assumed someone else had raised the alarm.

When Abby had returned to the pub, it had been well after midnight but she hadn't been able to sleep and so she'd sat down to write a feature article about the people she'd met since arriving in the small town.

"How are you feeling this morning?" Faith asked.

Before she could answer, the front door swung open and Detective Inspector Joshua Ryan strode in carrying a couple of coffees. Setting the coffees down, he dug inside his pocket and produced a doggie biscuit for Doyle.

"I have a full day ahead full of paperwork," he explained. "So, I thought I'd swing by and fortify myself with some of Joyce's coffee." He smiled at Abby. "So, are the girls giving you a farewell party or a welcome to Eden party tonight?"

"Oh, thanks for reminding me. I have to drop in on the Eden Thespians and see if they can outfit me with proper attire for the occasion. I hope they have a little bow tie for Doyle."

Doyle and Joshua exchanged a male bonding look.

Joshua handed her a piece of paper.

"What's this?" She skimmed through it and gasped.

"Really? You were actually serious about doing a background check on me?"

"Yes, and you'll be happy to note we're prepared to overlook that small infraction."

Faith jumped to her feet. "Let me see. What infraction? What did she do?"

Abby could not believe her ex had lodged a complaint about her slashing his favorite suit.

"I'm sure there's a story in there," Joshua said.

Abby folded the piece of paper and, smiling at Faith, said, "I'll tell you all about it tonight."

The door opened again and Sebastian Cavendish strode in. "I see someone beat me to it. I came to take you both out for morning coffee." He handed Abby an envelope.

Her marching orders?

He smiled and said, "I figured you needed a new contract."

~

Printed in Great Britain
by Amazon

63747782R00119